The UMBRELLA MOUSE

The
UMBRELLA
MOUSE

The
UMBRELLA
MOUSE

ANNA FARGHER

ILLUSTRATED BY SAM USHER

MACMILLAN CHILDREN'S BOOKS

Dedicated to Marie-Madeleine Fourcade,
Léon Faye and all the animals who bravely fight
for the lives of human beings.

First published 2019 by Macmillan Children's Books
an imprint of Pan Macmillan
20 New Wharf Road, London N1 9RR
Associated companies throughout the world
www.panmacmillan.com

ISBN 978-1-5290-0397-0

1 3 5 7 9 8 6 4 2

A CIP catalogue record for this book is available from
the British Library.

Typeset by Nigel Hazle
Printed and bound by CPI Group (UK) Ltd, Croydon CR0 4YY

CHAPTER ONE

JAMES SMITH & SONS
UMBRELLA SHOP, LONDON, 1944

The grandfather clock had just struck five when Pip Hanway saw Mr and Mrs Smith for the last time. Watching them closely, with her whiskers twitching on her cheeks, she peered out from under her umbrella canopy and tightened her tail around the end of one of its metal ribs, hoping more customers would soon visit the shop to tell more stories of the far-flung places she dreamed to see.

Mr Smith was standing behind the long mahogany counter, smiling at his wife as she dusted the umbrellas in the shop window. She fluttered from one umbrella to the next as the June sunlight poured inside, all the time having no idea that a small family of mice were secretly living inside her precious antique umbrella, occupying pride of place at the front of the display.

It had once belonged to the first man to use an umbrella in London, Jonas Hanway. His great-nephew donated it to the first James Smith over a hundred years before, and when Pip's father's family moved into the building shortly afterwards, they made the Hanway umbrella their home. They became the first English umbrella mice, so proud of their house and its owner that they named themselves after Jonas Hanway himself.

Nevertheless, if Mrs Smith had known they were there, Pip thought with a giggle that crinkled the fur on her nose, she would have pulled up her skirt around her knees, climbed on top of the shop counter and screeched like a kettle bubbling on the stove.

Pip and every other Hanway mouse before her had passed their days in the same way. As the red buses rumbled past the shop on Bloomsbury Street, Pip and her parents secretly nestled together, high up inside their umbrella where it was safe and dark, and when they weren't sleeping, watched customers come inside James Smith & Sons to buy Mr Smith's handmade umbrellas. The shop was always busy, despite the country being at war for the last five years.

'As long as there's rain, there's business!' Mr Smith would say, even when there was not a cloud in the sky.

'If we go back to Gignese in the summer we might melt like the ice cream,' Mrs Smith was saying for the second time that day.

'And you know how Peter hates feeling too hot.'

She had spoken about Gignese every breakfast, lunch and supper since their son Peter was sent to fight in Normandy three weeks before. The little Italian town had the only umbrella museum in the world and Mr and Mrs Smith had been planning to take the Hanway umbrella there for years to organize a special exhibition with the owner of the museum. When Peter came home at the end of the war, they were all going on holiday to see the museum again, high up in the northern Italian hills where they would eat vibrant food one could only dream of in wartime.

Pip grinned mischievously. Mr and Mrs Smith didn't know that the Hanway mice were joining them. It was going to be the first time Pip would meet her Italian aunts, uncles and cousins, who her mother had left behind on her own adventure to see the world. She had stowed away inside an antique lace parasol Mrs Smith had bought for her historical display inside the shop, and it was love at first sight when she arrived and bumped into Papa late one night, nibbling crumbs behind the kitchen bread bin.

'Did you hear that, Papa?' Pip squeaked excitedly. 'Ice cream!'

'Shhh!' Mama and Papa scolded from their nest of fluff and old newspaper, cleverly tucked away behind the top notch at the highest point inside the umbrella canopy.

And Pip knew why.

Many Hanway mice had been snapped in a trap, including their last surviving relative, Great-Aunt Marble, who could never resist one last bite of biscuit in the upstairs tea cupboard. Mrs Smith's ears were as sharp as a bat's and if she thought she heard the tiniest of squeaks, traps would be hidden throughout the shop and the flat above. But Pip didn't care how noisy she was. She'd never be stupid enough to end up like greedy Aunt Marble. Besides, ice cream and Peter were the best things she'd heard all day, especially after eating another dry crust of Mrs Smith's wartime loaf of bread.

The truth was that she missed Peter as much as Mr and Mrs Smith did, even if she had been scared he was going to kill her at first. The first time they met was late one night when she was secretly in his bedroom with her friends Dot and Joe, two black and white mice from the pub next door. Peter never would have known they were there if those two nitwits hadn't started bickering over who was the fastest mouse. When they knocked over a photo frame on Peter's bedside table, it crashed loudly on to the floor and suddenly he was wide awake, sitting bolt upright in bed.

At once, Pip had darted across the floor, knowing that if she didn't outrun him she would certainly die a horrible death. But Peter had been fast on his feet as he chased her downstairs to the shop. He was at her heels when she sprinted up the umbrella pole to safety, curling up beside her parents, who had still been fast asleep in their nest at the top of the canopy. Pip had trembled with terror at that moment, feeling sure she had led a monster straight to her family. But instead of hurting her, Peter had simply turned around and gone back to bed. Soon after, he started leaving crumbs under the umbrella when Mr and Mrs Smith weren't looking. Pip was always the first to find them, so her parents never suspected that Peter knew where they lived.

The last time Pip had seen Peter was the morning he had left to go to war, when he rescued her from the deep kitchen sink. She had slipped inside it and, hearing him come into the room, Dot and Joe had panicked and left her behind. He had gently cradled her in the palm of his hand and stroked her white underbelly before carefully putting her back beneath her umbrella. But Pip could never tell Mama and Papa about her adventure. Then they'd know she'd been sneaking out of the umbrella to explore while they slept.

'And we can't possibly leave the shop to go to Gignese in the autumn or spring – they're our busiest months,' Mrs Smith continued. 'And business is good in winter too, especially around Christmas.'

'When the war is over and Peter comes home,' Mr Smith said softly, walking to her and placing his arm around her shoulders. 'He won't mind what time of year we go.'

His voice had quivered with sadness, and he stopped to clear his throat before continuing. The truth was that even if Peter did find his way home, he would no longer be the same boy Mr and Mrs Smith knew. He was a man they could not protect from the cruelty of war, and those men didn't often go on holiday with their parents.

'And he'll be home soon, love,' Mr Smith said, tenderly kissing Mrs Smith's forehead, her eyes at once filling with tears. 'I can feel it in my bones.'

A knot of worry tightened in Pip's stomach. For the last three weeks, everyone who came into the shop had been talking about the D-Day landings in Normandy and how many thousands of soldiers had died in the battle there.

A brass bell jingled loudly as the front door to James Smith & Sons swung open and a young woman with brown hair tied back with a green ribbon stepped inside.

'Bedtime soon, Miss Pip,' Mama said from high up inside the umbrella. Pip's tail flicked irritably as she glanced up to see her mother busily fluffing their nest with her paws, 'It's late.'

'But Mama, I just want to see who this customer is.'

'All right, one more customer and I want no arguments when they leave.'

Why is it, Pip thought with a frustrated sigh, *that those few extra minutes before I'm meant to be in bed are always the most fun and quick to pass?* She hoped this girl was interesting and stayed a while.

'Good morning,' Mrs Smith said, approaching the young woman across the shop floor. 'Can I help you?'

'Hello,' she said, closing the door behind her with a final rattle from the bell. She smiled warmly. 'Yes, I would like to buy my father a birthday present.'

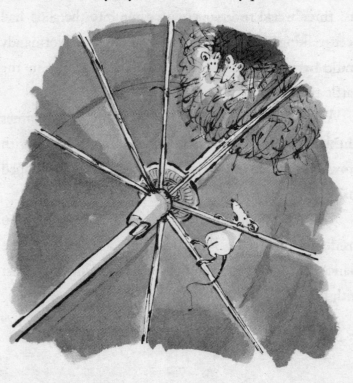

'We have a number o_____ do you think he would like _____ said, pointing to a plain wooden_____ nearby display. 'Or a carved one? W_____ animal heads if you think he would like _____

'How lovely,' the young woman sa__ _____ng delighted as she touched a tiger's head snarling from a timber handle. 'I think he'd like that. We used to go to the zoo all the time in Berlin.'

'Berlin? Goodness, are you a refugee? I never would have guessed. Your accent sounds completely English.'

'Yes, we had to leave Germany in 1933, when I was nine years old. If we had waited a day longer, the Gestapo would have arrested us.'

'Your family must have been terrified.'

'Yes, we were,' she said solemnly. 'My father is still on their blacklist for speaking out against the Nazi Party in the newspaper he used to write for. We escaped on the train and stayed in Switzerland and Paris before we arrived here in 1935.' She smiled to herself. 'It's funny. I must have lost my accent in the last nine years, although I have never forgotten my German or French.' She paused and shook her head sadly. 'We were very lucky. After all the terrible things that have happened in my can't imagine ever living there again. I

ngland is where I belong now.'

'And you're very welcome here, my dear,' Mr Smith said with a kind nod of his head.

'So is your father,' Mrs Smith said, nodding too. 'And as an honorary Englishman he really must have an umbrella. I'm afraid he may never get used to the cold and damp weather we have here, but a fine shelter from the rain will help.'

'You should try the winter in Berlin!' She laughed, turning back to the carved umbrella handles, her eyes narrowing slightly as she made her decision. 'I think he'd like that one with a mouse carving,' she said, pointing to it. 'It's his nickname for me, and he's always trying to catch them and set them free in the park.'

Pip let out a muffled squeak of joy. She always liked it when people picked the mice umbrellas.

'Very good choice,' Mrs Smith said. 'Shall I wrap it for you?'

'Yes, please.'

'Follow me,' she said, leading her to the far end of the shop's long mahogany counter. 'Which wrapping paper do you think your father would like?'

Behind them, the front door jangled open again as

another customer arrived and closed the door behind him. Recognizing the man taking off his fedora hat, Mr Smith briskly approached him while Mrs Smith chatted to the woman on the other side of the shop.

'Papa!' Pip cried with excitement, immediately remembering the man's stern, unremarkable face.

'Shhhh! Pip, for whiskers' sake!' Mama said.

'It's the spy man!' she whispered as loudly as she could. 'He must have come to collect the umbrellas we found in the downstairs workshop!'

'Let me have a look,' Papa said, eyes twinkling with enthusiasm.

Hastily clambering out of their nest and down the pole of the Hanway umbrella, Papa expertly hopped and jumped along its metal stretchers to meet Pip, wrapping his tail around the end of one of its metal ribs to peer out from under the canopy on to shop floor.

'It's a pleasure to see you again, sir,' Mr Smith said, warmly shaking the man's hand. 'Please wait here, I'll be back with your order in a moment.'

Mr Smith turned away and stepped behind the shop counter. As he disappeared through a swinging door that led to the downstairs workshop, the man patiently waited under the shop's butter-coloured signs. His eyes drifted over big Victorian lettering, which read 'James Smith & Sons Umbrellas', and the framed black and white photographs of Mr and Mrs Smith and their umbrella-manufacturing ancestors, proudly hanging on the wall behind the shop counter.

'It's definitely him,' Pip said, speaking rapidly.

She had been hoping to see this man again. There wasn't another customer like him. He had been in the shop a month ago and quietly given Mr Smith technical drawings to build three special umbrellas that Pip and her parents had then searched for in the downstairs workshop. Each had something very secret woven into its design. One handle separated from its umbrella pole to reveal a hidden blade of a sword, another had a pull-out poison bottle camouflaged in the hook, while the last umbrella had a secret button concealed in the ear of a carved-wood dog handle that burst its canopy open.

'You're right!' Papa whispered with a grin that creased the fur around his eyes. 'He'll be a member of Churchill's Secret Army, fighting to defeat the Axis Powers – only the very bravest souls survive. Most of the time, nobody knows who they are – they could be anyone from Peter to Father Christmas – and he'll be giving his special umbrellas to secret agents in Europe, probably the

French Resistance. Although a hidden button in an umbrella handle isn't that special, we have one on ours, look!' He proudly pointed a paw to one of the fig leaves carved into their umbrella handle. 'The King of Persia gave this to Jonas Hanway when he was on his travels there. It's very special to have a silver handle inlaid with gold, like ours.'

'Yes, yes, I know,' Pip interrupted, sullenly rolling her eyes with boredom. The last thing she felt like was the same old history lesson from Papa. 'Jonas Hanway the traveller and the charity man that built the hospitals, who was the first man to use an umbrella in London,' she said, huffily predicting what he was going to say. 'You've told me about him a million times. Mr and Mrs Smith waffle on about him every chance they get as well.'

'Knowing how you got your name and your home is no boring matter, young Pip,' Papa said angrily, his whiskers drooping with hurt. 'Your great-great-great-great-great-grandfather took Hanway for our family name because he admired Jonas Hanway for all the kindness he showed to those worse off than him. That's something to be proud of. Furthermore, this umbrella is one of the first to be used in England. Just think how common they are now! You live in a piece of history! Not only that – your family has been inside this umbrella since James Smith & Sons Umbrella Shop was built over a hundred years ago. That's rare, my girl.'

'I know how important our home is Papa!' she snapped, her hackles bristling with impatience. 'You tell me the same stupid story all the time!'

'Right. Enough of that temper, Pip!' Mama said firmly, standing by their nest with her paws on her hips. 'You're tired. It's time for bed now.'

'Just one more minute, Mama,' she protested, craning her neck to see Mr Smith hand the man a long parcel wrapped in brown paper, tied with string.

After shaking Mr Smith's hand, the man turned to the shop's front door. Pulling it towards him with a clang from the bell, he paused to hold it open for the young woman, smiling gratefully as she passed through it with her father's birthday present tucked under her arm. After giving a brief, official-looking nod, the man put his fedora hat back on his head, stepped into the sunshine and faded into the endless crowd walking up and down Bloomsbury Street.

'No,' Mama said. 'The shop will still be here tonight when it's safe for us to go outside.'

'But there won't be any customers.'

'They'll come again tomorrow morning. You can listen to more of their stories then.'

'Come on, madam,' Papa said in a tone that Pip knew was pointless to argue with. Besides, all the customers had left now and she couldn't think of another excuse to stay up longer. The shop would be closing soon. 'Off we go.'

Hopping from one metal umbrella stretcher to another, they scaled the pole to their nest. Pip yawned loudly, knowing that if she behaved now, Mama and Papa would never suspect her of sneaking out of the umbrella once they were asleep. Then she'd be free to listen to whomever she liked and explore whatever part of James Smith & Sons Umbrella Shop she wanted, so long as she stayed out of sight. She smiled to herself excitedly as she curled into a little ball beside them and rested one of her big ears against Mama's soft, furry chest. Pip was soon asleep, but years of practice meant she was wide awake again a few hours later. She listened to the even, fluttering thud of her mother's heartbeat, and waited for the gentle rumble of her parents' snores, before she silently sneaked back down the umbrella pole to watch the customers come into the shop once more.

The grandfather clock clunked mechanically, as if it was clearing its throat, and Mrs Smith glanced at its handsome brass face as its familiar melody began to strike five o'clock. It was just before it finished playing the Westminster Chimes that it happened. As if from nowhere, a terrible crash thundered through the shop, and nothing was ever the same again.

CHAPTER TWO

FIRE

In one furious snarl, Pip's life as she knew it came to an end. The bomb struck Bloomsbury Street like lightning and belched its insides outwards in a hot, black cloud that swallowed the sun. At first, the street held its breath as the dust hung like fog in the air. Smouldering papers and photographs fell from the sky like autumn leaves tumbling in a breeze. Mr and Mrs Smith's cherished wedding picture came to rest on the front step of where James Smith & Sons Umbrellas had once stood. Above it, there was no longer a door to welcome customers inside. The shop was lying as helpless as a house of cards, blown to pieces by a careless player.

Deep beneath the mangled bricks and broken glass, little Pip Hanway opened her eyes in the dark.

'Mama!' she coughed. 'Papa!'

But only a dull roar bellowed in her ears. Searching the shadows in alarm, she realized she was alone in a small hollow in the rubble. There was no way in and no way out.

'Mama! Papa!' she cried again, but all she heard was ringing and the sound of her little heart clamouring inside her head.

Pip trembled. She had never been completely alone before. Even when she secretly crept outside the umbrella and into the umbrella shop, Mama and Papa had always been sleeping nearby.

'MAMA! PAP—'

At that moment,
the earth rumbled
above her and dust
poured into the hollow,
rushing around her
ankles to her knees.
Pip threw her head
from side to side,
desperately trying
to stop the dust
creeping inside her

mouth and nose. Suddenly the earth shook violently again. At once, the darkness overhead cracked into a jagged web of light. With a racing heart, Pip hurried through a tiny opening like thread passing through the eye of a needle and chased the slivers of daylight to the street above.

But the world Pip laid eyes on was not the world she knew. Sirens wailed and men and women ran frantically past buildings that were stripped of their walls and windows. Once private places were now rooms on public display. She shuddered at a painting dangling lopsided in

an upstairs bedroom, hanging perilously above a floor that had been blown away. The number eight bus to Bethnal Green that normally stopped in front of the umbrella shop was now standing crippled in the middle of the road with smoke billowing out of jagged, broken windows. It was then that a terrible shiver of panic threw Pip's eyes wide open. Ahead of her, the half-closed Hanway umbrella lay beneath the bus's front tyre, rippling with a smouldering, ebony glow.

Pip's legs trembled with terror. Clambering over shattered bricks and glass twenty times her size, she reached the road and sprinted for the umbrella, zigzagging through the enormous boots and high-heeled shoes that were chaotically crashing across her path. A few moments brought her to the bus, moaning as it buckled in the heat and spat flame and smoke that curled her whiskers as if she had crawled into an open fire.

'Mama! Papa!' she cried, reaching for the umbrella. She yelped in pain as her paws flinched and blistered on its tarpaulin. With beads of sweat racing down her brow, Pip desperately searched for a way inside to find Mama and Papa, but it was hopeless. The umbrella was heavier and hotter than anything she had ever known.

'Looks like you're in spot of bovver, aren't ya, mate?

These new doodlebugs don't do things by 'alves.'

Standing there in the smoke, with a long pink tongue lolling out of his mouth, was a small dog with a kind, sandy face, dark eyes and short, black fur like worn-out toothbrush bristles. Wrapped around his body was a grubby white coat with a thick red cross stitched on the side. Instantly Pip's heart jumped with hope. He was one of the search and rescue dogs Mama and Papa had told her about. They followed their noses and found people buried under rubble after the bombs fell. She had seen one trot past the shop window once, walking with a man dressed in dark blue overalls and a white tin hat.

'Help!' Pip cried. 'Please help! My Mama and Papa are inside!'

The dog snapped the umbrella in his mouth, but it burned his lips and he spat it out with a growl. Panting in the heat, he carefully scampered around the umbrella. Jabbing it quickly and lightly with his coal black nose, he found its silver tip. Pinching it with his teeth, the terrier shuffled backwards and dragged it away from the bus into a nearby puddle next to a fire engine. It hit the water with a hiss.

'Careful, mate!' the dog said, watching stunned as

Pip swiftly paddled across the water.

'Mama!' she cried breathlessly, dragging her sopping wet body out of the puddle. 'Papa!'

Frantically racing inside the hot umbrella, she hurried to their nest at the highest point of the canopy. The place where they had spent their days curled up together, hiding from the outside world. But the nest was gone. Only a few stray pieces of fluff and old newspaper remained.

She called again, coughing in the stifling heat as she scrambled around the umbrella, searching every pleat, pocket and furrow inside the canopy. 'Where are you?'

A sick feeling of fear crept over her. Still she looked and her nose twitched with hope as she lifted each ripple of tarpaulin in her paws, desperately wanting to find them tucked inside a fold. But each one felt emptier than the last and soon a horrible screech of panic rang inside her ears.

Mama and Papa were not inside the umbrella.

'Where's yer mum? Where's yer dad?' the dog yapped, poking his nose into the end of the umbrella and sniffing vigorously. 'This ain't a place for little 'uns!'

But Pip didn't know where they were. Closing her

eyes, she wrapped herself up in the dark creases of the umbrella and pressed her nose against the canopy, searching for Mama and Papa's fading smell.

In her heart she knew she had lost them.

CHAPTER THREE

SEARCH AND RESCUE

'Now, none of that, love. I can't bear to see a nipper cry,' the terrier said, lying on his stomach with his legs splayed out behind him and his chin resting sympathetically just inside the umbrella canopy.

Pip crawled into a little ball and wept, longing for Mama and Papa to come back. Human screaming and yelling echoed all around and she clasped her paws over her ears, trying to think of a way to escape the nightmare unfolding outside.

'You count your blessings on a day like today,' the dog said. 'This bleedin' war ain't been as kind to many – some of us don't even have a roof over our heads these days.'

A crash sounded nearby and the dog whipped his head out of the umbrella with his ears pricked high on his head. A moment later, Pip gasped, feeling him drag the umbrella across the ground with his teeth.

'Dickin!' a man cried, following it with a long whistle that went up a note at the end. 'Dickin! Come here, boy!'

'You stay put, love,' the terrier said, giving the umbrella one last push with his nose, hiding it in a gap under a splintered bedroom door lying against the rubble. 'It ain't safe for ya out here and I've got a job to do. Don't worry, I won't forget about you. If I find yer mum and dad, I promise I'll bring them straight here.'

A prickly feeling of isolation crept over Pip as the sound of Dickin's claws scratching against the pavement disappeared. Taking her paws away from her ears and lifting her head, the bombsite sounded less frightening, like it was in a next-door room. But she couldn't stay here. She *had* to find Mama and Papa and get herself and the umbrella away from this place.

Uncurling herself from her ball, she crept out of the canopy. She ran her paws across the carvings scored into the length of the umbrella handle and wrapped her arms around its hook. She tugged with all her might, but it remained rooted to the ground. With tears filling her eyes, Pip knew moving the umbrella on her own was impossible. A terrible choice tied a knot inside her stomach as she slowly edged away, risking losing it forever to search for Mama and Papa.

The fallen door created a shadowy opening, framing the early-evening horror on Bloomsbury Street as though she viewed it through a secret window. Scanning the ground for Mama and Papa, she was mesmerized, watching firemen wrestle with a hose and soak the smouldering bus with a jet of white water. To their left, men and women rushed about the debris, wearing navy-blue overalls and dark metal hats with bright 'W's printed on the front. Some carried sobbing children in their arms while others helped stunned people coated in dust to clamber over the rubble. Behind them, Pip spied Dickin scampering over slabs of stone and planks of wood, following his nose and wagging his tail.

Suddenly the terrier yapped and began frantically digging. A tall, dark-haired man wearing black-rimmed spectacles and a white metal hat raced to his side, beckoning other air-raid wardens to join him. As a group, the men and women rolled away heavy blocks of bricks still cemented together and, reaching into the hole, they pulled out a young boy, unmoving as if he was asleep. A moment later, a nurse in a tin hat with a cream apron tied around her pale-blue dress rushed to meet them, leading an ambulance man and woman carrying a stretcher. Gently placing the boy upon it, they hurried away.

After giving Dickin quick congratulatory pats on his head, the air-raid wardens scattered, resuming their search for those in need. The terrier's pink tongue lolled out of his mouth in a smile before he leaped back across the collapsed buildings, sniffing the debris with his black, shiny nose.

Pip's heart was in her mouth as she watched the dog's sharp sense of smell lead him and the air-raid wardens to three more people and two cats trapped under the rubble. Each time he yapped, she willed him to uncover Mama and Papa, but each time he saved somebody else, and the flutter of hope inside her grew faint. She had to do something to help.

'Mama!' she cried, stepping out from under the fallen door into the open air with her paws cupped around her mouth. 'Papa!'

'No!' Dickin barked, snapping his head in the direction of her voice. His ears flattened against his head with worry, seeing her wander into the road. 'Get back under the door!'

Pip continued, tears swimming in her eyes. Over her

shoulder, ambulance doors slammed shut one after another as two medics rushed into the front seats of the vehicle. A moment later, it roared into life with a rev of its engine, screeching straight towards her.

'Look out!' Dickin yapped, now bounding across the rubble.

The terrier sprang across the street. Rocketing into Pip, they somersaulted between the ambulance wheels. The vehicle hurtled over them as it rushed along the road. Tumbling together, Pip and Dickin landed heavily against the fallen door.

'What are you doing?' Pip scowled, struggling to stand. 'I have to find my parents.'

'Don't be an idiot,' Dickin growled. 'You're lucky you're not stuck to them tyres like glue. I told you to stay put!'

'I can't sit here doing nothing.'

'I think it's high time you told me yer name and I took yer somewhere safe.'

'I-I'm Pip,' she stammered. She'd never been introduced to any dog before, let alone an important one, like he was. 'Pip Hanway.'

'Pleased to meet ya, Pip. My name's Dickin, as you've probably heard these folks shouting. I'm a search and rescue dog and I'm here to help. It's not safe for you here right now.'

'But I can't leave,' she said, desperation thumping in her chest. 'What if Mama and Papa come back?'

'I ain't got a whiff of yer mum and dad yet. I'll do my best to find 'em, but ya got to promise me that you'll stay under this door.'

'But what if—'

'No what ifs, mate. You've got to trust me and that's that.'

Pip stared into his scruffy black face. He must be a good sort if he was a real search and recuse dog and he had already done a lot to help her, and everybody else trapped under the rubble too.

'All right.' She nodded reluctantly. 'But I'm keeping a lookout for Mama and Papa while you're gone.'

'Deal. Now you get back under that door,' he said, wagging his tail and nudging her with his cold, wet nose. 'I'll see ya as soon as I finish my shift.'

CHAPTER FOUR

DICKIN

The sun had already risen in a pink mackerel sky when the terrier returned, caked in grey dust from the tips of his whiskers to the end of his tail. Flopping on his side by Pip, who was still peering out from the opening under the fallen door, he rested his head by her paws and panted with his tongue hanging out of the corner of his mouth. All night, Pip hadn't taken her eyes off him as he tirelessly searched through the ruins of Bloomsbury Street. The din of panic had subsided now and the road was quiet as if it was resting from the trauma of the hours before. Dotted around the rubble, the air-raid wardens talked quietly among themselves, sipping tea from white mugs between bites of fresh sandwiches cut into triangles. The tall man wearing black-rimmed spectacles stood by a camouflage-green van with 'WVS' printed on its bonnet, which was parked at the side of the road. A woman leaned out a through a large hatch cut into the van's side. Taking a handful of bread from her, the tall man turned away and approached Dickin in broad strides.

'There you go, boy. You deserve this,' he said, placing the food by the terrier's head and affectionately rubbing between his ears. Pip darted back under the door and hid in the shadows of the umbrella. Giving the bread a sniff, Dickin turned flat on his stomach and wolfed it down where he lay. 'Stay here and rest,' the man said, walking to the other air-raid men and women once more. 'That was quite a shift for the both of us.'

'Help yourself, love.' The terrier said, nudging the last mouthful of food under the fallen door with a wag of his tail. 'You must be hungry if you ain't slept all night.'

'Where are my mama and papa?' Pip said, not giving the bread a glance.

Dickin's tail fell limp. Her brow, furrowed with hope, was a look he saw every time the bombs fell. Those lost, longing faces broke his heart.

'I hate to be the one to tell ya this,' he said, gently shaking his head. 'But if we could have, we would have found them by now. It's time I took ya somewhere

where you'll be well looked after now.'

'I can't leave. Mama and Papa always come back, I have to wait for them. They would never leave me.'

'I'm sorry, love, but don't you reckon they'd have found ya by now? We ain't moved all night. And look around ya . . .' Pip's eyes followed his, sombrely falling on newly organized piles of rubble and skeletons of buildings pummelled into unnatural, jagged shapes by the bomb blast. 'Most of this site's been cleared. If they were trapped under what little there is left of this place, they would've climbed out and found ya.'

'But they have to find me,' Pip whimpered.

'They're in a place they can't come back from.' Dickin paused and his gruff voice cracked with sadness, his scruffy head between his paws. 'They're dead.'

Pip suddenly felt so unsteady on her legs that a soft breeze could have carried her far away. How could they be dead when she had just been curled up beside them in their nest, resting her ears on Mama's chest, listening to her heartbeat? It was impossible to think she would never see them again.

'No,' Pip said, standing tall and defiant on her hind paws. 'I don't believe you. If you're not going to find them, then I will!'

She dashed from under the fallen door to the solitary front step where James Smith & Sons Umbrellas had stood, too devastated to care about being seen by the humans standing on the other side of the street.

'Now, Pip,' Dickin said urgently, leaping up to follow her. 'There ain't any need to look over there.'

Pip quickened her pace, determined to search under every crushed brick and splintered piece of wood whether the dog liked it or not. But as she neared the step, her throat tightened with sorrow. A sheer drop lay before her and she looked down into the deep, dark, jagged mouth of a crater which had replaced the welcoming shop floor where she had last seen Mama and Papa sleeping inside their umbrella.

'It was a direct hit, love.' Dickin said softly, peering into the ruins beside her. 'It's a miracle you made it out alive.'

Pip couldn't speak. Mama and Papa moved fast and could squeeze through the tiniest of spaces. She'd never seen anything they couldn't hop and climb over. She looked at the remains of the umbrella shop and a sick feeling of despair choked her breath. Crawling out of the mangled bricks, wood and glass wouldn't have posed a problem for them.

Turning away, her eyes rested on a pool of dried blood on the pavement, still outlining the shape of where a human body had lain. Mr and Mrs Smith must be dead too, and poor Peter fighting the war in France would have no idea. It was then that a tremor of regret shook her chest. Before they had gone to bed inside their nest, she had been so mean to Papa. She would do anything to go back and say she was sorry, tell him she loved him, listen to his history stories and rest her head on Mama's shoulder one last time. Drawing a long shuddering breath, a terrible, painful loneliness she had never felt before gripped her heart.

'I know it's hard, love,' Dickin said with a kind nudge of his scruffy head. 'Come on, let's get ya back to yer umbrella where it's safe. They may be dopey with no sleep but we can't risk them humans catchin' sight of ya. They're a jumpy bunch when they see little 'uns like you. Loony behaviour if ya ask me. Here,' he said, throwing her up on to his snout with his cold, wet nose. She flopped on it, feeling paralysed by grief. 'You must be as tired as a bee after everythin' you've been through.'

Reaching the umbrella, he shuffled his head under the fallen door with his tail in the air. Sliding from his nose, Pip crawled into a little ball beside it with tears soaking her furry cheeks.

'This bleedin' war took my family from me too,' the dog continued softly, lying on his stomach and resting his head next to her with a whimper of sympathy. Pip quietly listened, feeling comforted by his deep, gruff voice. 'It weren't a big one – just my Jack and his mum since his pa went off to war – but I'd have done anythin' for them. We were so happy until we found out Jack had to move to the countryside where kids would be safer. The East End of London was in a bit o' strife, you see. Even with blackouts every night, Hitler's bombers found us cos of the Thames shinin' in the moonlight, and there ain't no point bombin' a field of potatoes, now is there?

'In the end, Jack's mum arranged for us all to go,' Dickin continued. 'She quit her factory job and called her Auntie Dora in Cornwall. We'd have to pull our weight on the farm, she said, but we'd get a roof over our heads and maybe a fresh egg or two and you can't get many of them in London these days, mate.

'That evenin' I lay in my kennel with that fluttery feelin' in my stomach, thinkin' of all them rabbits I was gonna chase, maybe even a sheep or two if I was lucky. But then somethin' stopped my daydreamin'. A bleedin' fox was nosin' around our cabbages! There's nothin' I like more than chasin' one of them out the garden and I gave it the run of its life, snappin' at its heels all the way into Vicky Park.

'Then out of nowhere, somethin' strange tickled me whiskers like a thunderstorm was comin'. Suddenly, Moanin' Minnie's siren started wailin' and a terrible feelin' shook inside me. I wasn't with Jack or his mum to get them into the Anderson shelter. I'd left them back at the house, asleep in their beds.

'A sound like an angry beehive started filling the sky and a minute later the great crashin' started. I sprinted home faster than I'd ever run before. There weren't a star or a moon in the sky, just a red glow above London, like it was bleedin'. All I could see was flames and smoke. Humans ran around, shoutin' for help, screamin' for water, and all the streets I knew were gone. When I found my house, I was too late. All that was left was a big pile of bricks.

'I couldn't hear my Jack and our mum with them bombs bangin' all about the place, but nothin' stops my nose. That's when I dug up his specs, all cracked, bent and sticky like they'd been dipped in red treacle.

'The next day, men came and took their bodies away

in one of them green ambulance vans. They drove away without givin' me a second glance and I chased it till my legs gave way and I fell in the street, tryin' to breathe. I went back to where I found Jack's specs and lay next to them, still smelling my Jack and our mum, but I knew they'd never come home.

'Then one day, a lump of bread rolled across the ground by my paws. A man wearin' one of them metal hats crouched next to me with a sandwich in one hand and a cuppa tea in the other.

'"So much for the 'phoney war' eh?" he said, throwin' me another bit of crust, but I was too sad to eat. "Not hungry?" he said, scratchin' that sweet spot behind my ears so's I couldn't stop my leg scratchin' the ground. "Nor me, pal."

'Before me stood a bloke, tall and lanky with black-rimmed specs just like my Jack. He came every day to clear the mess from my street with other wardens and I grew fond of them. On his last day, he asked me to go home with him.

'"There ain't nothin' left for us here now, boy," he said, and he was right.

'You see, love, that was the end of my last life, but my new one ain't bad and I bet yours will be all right too.

Mr King and me are family now. He looks out for me and I look out for him. I couldn't save my Jack or his mum and Mr King couldn't save his family neither. So what I'm sayin' is that there're lots of us like you. We're all in it together and it's somethin' like this that brings us all closer. You'll see it too, mate, I promise ya. And I'm sure your folks'd want ya to be safe. It's time for you to start your new life now, just like I did.'

'I won't leave the umbrella!' Pip snapped, locking eyes with the terrier as her hackles rose. She glowered, desperately hoping her fury would squash her sorrow. 'My family has never been without it, I will not leave it here!'

'It's all right,' Dickin said softly. 'Don't worry, we can take it with us. But we have to leave this place. Have ya got any other friends or family I can take ya to?'

Pip looked at where James Smith & Sons used to be. Trembling, she cast her eyes on the pub next door, where Dot and Joe had lived. Nothing was left of it either.

'I don't have anyone,' she said. 'Everyone I knew was here and now they're all . . .'

'It's all right, mate, don't you worry,' Dickin said. 'There's a place for folks like you. It's called St Giles.'

'I've heard of St Giles.' She remembered Mama and

Papa had grimaced whenever they heard the name. 'It's full of beggars and thieves.'

'I wouldn't take ya there if it weren't safe. St Giles is the place to go when you ain't got a place to go, and in wartime that ain't somethin' to sniff at.'

Pip looked at the umbrella and thought of Mama and Papa. They would have hated it if they ended up there. There had to be another place.

'Wait!' she said, and at once her whiskers popped upright with an idea. 'I know where I'm meant to go!'

'Good. Where is it? I'll take ya there.'

'I'm going to the umbrella museum in Gignese. It's right in the north of Italy.'

'Italy?' Dickin scoffed. 'You must be crackers! Even after the Allied invasion of the south, northern Italy is still enemy territory!'

'But I have nowhere else to go,' Pip said, fighting the tears swimming in her eyes. 'I am the last surviving Hanway mouse of Bloomsbury Street, but my mother is from Gignese. I have family there. We were going to visit them when Mr and Mrs Smith took the umbrella to show the owners of the museum. It belonged to Jonas Hanway.' Pip's voice cracked. She could almost hear Papa telling her about her family and the umbrella where she and her ancestors had lived for over a hundred years. 'He was the first man to use an umbrella in England. Before him, people had to get horse-drawn carriages when it rained. I come from a long line of umbrella mice and my umbrella belongs in a museum. I have to take it with me.'

'That's fair enough, mate, but how are you plannin' on gettin' there? There's crossin' the English Channel, *and* there's travellin' across Europe, which is at war, in case you hadn't noticed.' The terrier shook his head. 'No offence, Pip, but you're one little mouse. I'd sooner see Winston Churchill put on a dress and dance in the fountains at Trafalgar Square.'

'All we ever wanted was to go to Gignese to meet my mother's family and see where she grew up. A place in the Italian hills that's filled with important umbrellas, far away from the bombs in London and . . .' Her voice faltered and, with furious grief, she clenched her paws into fists, stared into Dickin's flabbergasted face and cried out in a crescendo: 'Wouldn't you do anything to go to the place where you had some family left? Where you know you are meant to be? I don't know how I'll get there, but I'll never know unless I try. I just need to find the courage in my heart to begin something new!'

On uttering the same words Mama always used to say when she was struggling, Pip realized she would never hear her or Papa's voices again. She would never tickle her whiskers together with theirs and see them smile. She would never rest her ears on Mama's soft, furry chest and listen to her heartbeat before she went to sleep. No longer able to fight the sadness bellowing in her heart, tears raced down Pip's cheeks and travelled the lengths of her whiskers before hitting the ground in small thuds.

Dickin fell silent. He had to admit, there was truth in what Pip said. He'd do anything and everything to be near his family again. All he had left of them was their gravestones in a Poplar churchyard, and he let nothing stop him from going there whenever he could.

'Well,' he said with a sigh. 'You can't do it on your own, that's for sure. I can't believe I'm sayin' this, but I think I know someone that could help ya.'

'What?' Pip gasped, looking up. 'Who?'

'I'll tell ya on the way,' the terrier said, energetically wagging his tail. 'Climb up and grab hold of me collar. I'm gonna help you find them.'

'Really?'

'Yes, and it's time we got a move on, we've been here

long enough,' he said, dipping his head and shoulders to the ground. 'Come on, love. This ain't time for dilly-dallying.'

With a lump in her throat, Pip nervously clutched Dickin's black, wiry fur in both paws and clambered up to the back of his neck.

'Now you hold on tight, Pip Hanway!' he said in a muffled voice as he took the umbrella between his teeth. 'This is gonna be the run of your life!'

CHAPTER FIVE

THE UNDERGROUND

Dickin bounded forward, zigzagging around the splintered wood, pummelled bricks and broken glass now gathered in heaps at the foot of the blasted buildings along Bloomsbury Street. Tightly clutching the scruff of his neck, Pip tearfully looked over her shoulder for one last glimpse of the remains of the umbrella shop. Leaving it behind felt as unnatural and terrifying as if she was losing the whiskers on her cheeks or the ears on her head. She had never known a moment without Mama and Papa or the shop, and as Dickin raced passed the enormous, charred black skeleton of the number eight bus in the middle of the road, Pip felt haunted by the flames that had flickered around the people inside.

Dickin forked sharply right on to Tottenham Court

Road and ran headlong into a flurry of people on their morning walk to work. Startled, the terrier suddenly darted between a young woman's legs. Shrieking in alarm, she fell to the pavement with a thump, sending a nearby newspaper stand tumbling on its side. A tall pile of papers – with *Hitler's Vengeance* printed in thick black letters across the top – scattered across the pavement. People gasped and helped the woman to her feet as Dickin galloped past them down a steep flight of stairs leading to the Underground. He raced across the ticketing hall to a closed door. Pip scrunched up her eyes and tightened her grip on Dickin's fur, waiting for the dog's body to crumple against the timber. But at the last moment, Dickin leaped upwards and threw all his weight into his front paws. The door burst open and instantly swung closed behind them.

Without a moment's hesitation, Dickin hurried down the spiralling metal staircase in front of them. Warm, stuffy air struck them in the face, as if they were passing through a veil of cobwebs, and a long-winded screech cried in the distance, followed by a gust of wind. At the bottom of the stairs, Dickin doubled back and scurried beneath the bottom steps. A greasy black metal grate sat at the foot of a wall covered in grubby cream tiles. Briefly dropping the umbrella on the ground, Dickin lifted the corner of the grate with his teeth and awkwardly pushed himself, Pip and the umbrella inside.

'Blimey,' Dickin panted in the stuffy gloom, gently placing the umbrella on the narrow metal floor. 'A chicken could lay hard boiled eggs in here.'

'Where are we going?' Pip said, a mixture of fear and excitement turning somersaults inside her chest.

'Don't worry, it ain't much further now,' he said, glancing back over his shoulder and giving her a reassuring wink. Nudging the umbrella with his nose, the terrier shuffled on his stomach along the narrow vent, which disappeared in a steep, dark descent just ahead. 'Hang on tight,' he said, his eyes twinkling in the half-light. 'Here we go!'

They plunged into the darkness. Scrunching up her

eyes, Pip let out a little yelp, feeling her whiskers pulling on her face with the force of the fall. Reaching the bottom with a bump but allowing no time for himself or the little mouse on his back to catch their breath, Dickin snapped up the umbrella between his teeth and sprinted along train tracks glinting through the shadows of a tall, domed, brick tunnel. A few paces later, he came to a stop beside an amber glow coming from a small hole where a number of bricks were missing from the wall. Distant chatter floated through the gap.

'All right, mate,' he panted, speaking quickly and dropping the umbrella to the ground. 'Get down and go inside.'

As Pip carefully clambered down from the terrier's neck to the cold, dusty earth by his front paws, a high-pitched screech sounded in the distance behind them. With it, a warm breeze started collecting around her whiskers.

'Where are we?' she said, peering into the opening. 'What's in there?'

'That's St Giles,' Dickin said, quietly bristling with impatience as Pip watched a puddle shimmering in the glow from the wall. Suddenly, a low growl rumbled in the dog's throat and his ears drew back angrily on his head. 'Come on, mate, we haven't got all day!'

His gruff and insistent bark loudly reverberated in the tunnel. Leaping in surprise, Pip looked up at him with a scowl. It was then that she understood why he was angry. Behind the terrier, two tiny white dots were growing larger inside the tunnel. The domed ceiling was becoming brighter and the ground beneath her paws was beginning to shake. Pip shuddered. A vast, wide-open jaw of light was greedily swallowing the gloom and storming along the train tracks towards them.

'Hurry up!' Dickin barked again, snatching the umbrella between his teeth and jumping up after Pip as she rushed through the hole. A clang sounded as the terrier stumbled to a standstill.

'Come on!' Pip said, feeling the tremors of the approaching train quake her little body. 'Hurry!'

Leaping forward once more, Dickin snarled in frustration. Again he tried, but it was hopeless. He could not push himself and the umbrella inside.

'Quick! Pip cried, helplessly watching him falter as the world now thrashed wildly from side to side. She gasped in horror. A white halo of light was quickly glowing brighter around her only friend in the world, carrying everything she had. 'Dickin!'

But the terrible screech of wheels racing across metal drowned out her yell. Wide-eyed with terror, the terrier turned and faced the oncoming light. At that moment, the silver tip of the umbrella slipped through the opening. Without thinking, Pip threw her paws around it and pulled with all her strength, just as Dickin hurled himself and the umbrella inside. Colliding, they tumbled across the ground and landed in a heap inside the opening in the wall. The train thundered past and disappeared, leaving the dog and the mouse lying petrified side by side, panting with terror and relief.

'Are you all right?' Dickin said. Clambering unsteadily to four paws, he shook the fright from the tip of his nose to the end of his tail. The little mouse didn't stir. 'Can you hear me, love? Are you OK?'

'No, I'm not all right,' Pip said, her lips trembling. 'I want to go home.'

'Wherever you are in this world now, mate, you're home,' Dickin said frankly as he tenderly nudged her to her paws with his nose. 'Come on, let's get you and this bleedin' umbrella to Gignizzy or wherever it is . . .'

'*Gignese*,' Pip said firmly, correcting him in the same bossy way Mama used to when she said something wrong. 'My new home is inside the umbrella museum in Gignese.'

'Right,' Dickin said, with his tongue lolling out of his mouth in a smile. 'That's just what I said.'

CHAPTER SIX

ST GILES

'So this is St Giles?' Pip said, looking about her and feeling a mixture of animal scents tingle her nose. They stood in a large chamber, separated from the Underground train tracks by a vast wall that disappeared high into the shadows above them. Eight dusty old bricks lay in disarray on the inside of the opening, crumbling around the edges where the mortar had been nibbled away.

'This is one of the secret entrances into it, yeah,' Dickin said. 'When war broke out we needed a place to hide from the humans. There ain't a food ration for pets so they started to do away with us to make sure there'd be enough to go around. And then when them bombs came knockin', it wasn't just humans that needed shelter, us animals needed a safe place below ground too.'

'But it isn't safe.' Pip frowned. 'That train nearly flattened us both.'

'You ain't wrong there, mate.' Dickin sighed, sad to see her frightened. 'I'm sorry about that. Sometimes danger crops up when you least expect it, but without it we'd never test our mettle. You did very well, if ya ask me,' he smiled. 'Come on, I'll show ya around.'

Carrying the umbrella between his teeth, Dickin trotted ahead in the half-light along a well-trodden path. The amber glow Pip had seen from the tracks was seeping over a steep decline, like honey spread over warm buttered bread. From down the hill, Pip could hear the sound of chattering creatures busily murmuring to each other, and the smell of sweet and savoury foods tickled her nose.

'Come on,' Dickin said, his grin still making his eyes smile despite the umbrella in his mouth. 'Let's go and find a nice cuppa tea.'

With a wag of his tail, the terrier promptly bounced ahead and disappeared down the steep slope into St Giles. Feeling the flutter of nerves tremble in her stomach, Pip hurried forward.

'How did all this get here?' Pip said, looking wide-eyed at a bustling market below.

'We have the St Giles Church mice to thank for that,' Dickin replied, sitting on his haunches at the edge of the market, the umbrella on the ground in front of him, patiently waiting for her to join him. 'When they saw what was going on, they enlisted the sewer rats and Tube mice to search for a place big enough for us animals to shelter in times of need. They know subterranean London better than anybody and they're the ones who gnawed the mortar between the bricks inside the train tunnel wall so we could get inside. And that ain't the only way in. They opened a whole lot of secret doors so we can use the sewers and abandoned chambers like this one. And no human's gonna risk their lives nosin' around busy Underground train tracks to notice us. We're as safe as houses down here.'

The market was filled with every small creature imaginable, from small stray dogs, rabbits, guinea pigs, mice and rats to sparrows, pigeons, frogs, toads, voles and weasels, all intermingling together, haggling at market stalls, sipping on drinks and nibbling on food. Everything was illuminated by rows of the little white lights Pip remembered hanging in the umbrella shop at Christmas, and almost every animal turned and whispered to their neighbours as the terrier padded past them with the umbrella clasped between his teeth. Some curiously pointed their paws and feathers at them, others had their heads hung too low to notice. Their whiskers drooped from their cheeks as if they carried the weight of the world. Like Pip, they had survived the bomb blast the day before and were new arrivals in St Giles.

'Make yer life a little brighta!' a market seller bellowed from somewhere in the crowd. 'Meat and pickled eggs! Sellin' fast! Last chance to buy!'

'Sugar! Butter!' Another cried nearby. 'Get yer sugar and yer butter 'ere!'

'Mama always wanted more butter and sugar,' Pip said to Dickin as they walked through the crowd, 'but she could never get it if the humans in our house didn't have any. How come there's so much here?'

'In wartime,' Dickin said, his voice muffled by the umbrella in his mouth, 'things like butter and sugar are in short supply. It's rationed so humans get their fair share – even the royal family has to make do. Us animals just get the scraps of what's left. But these dodgy dealers steal it straight from the human black market and then they sell it to them blightas down here that want it bad enough. Charge a pretty penny for it too.' A low growl rumbled in his throat. 'Thievin' sods. Don't look them in the eye or they'll try it on with ya.'

Pip looked away, but she couldn't resist quickly glancing back over her shoulder. She'd never seen a dodgy dealer before. At the same moment, a large toad with warts bubbling over his skin looked up from behind his stall. His steely yellow eyes caught her gaze, sending a cold shudder rippling over her fur. Gasping with horror, she snapped her head forward and quickened her pace alongside Dickin.

'Tea!' another seller shrieked into the crowd, 'Fre-esh tea! Soothe yer weary hearts! Come and get yer tea here!'

'What'cha reckon, mate?' Dickin said. 'I think we deserve one of them.'

The terrier eagerly trotted forwards to the stall. Gently laying the umbrella on the ground alongside it, he sat on his haunches and loomed over the counter with a customary sniff. The stall was made from small, scuffed matchboxes stacked one on top of the other. Each box had 'BRITISH MADE' printed in big letters across the front and some had pictures of boats and army men as big as Pip. With her little nose twitching, she wobbled on her tiptoes and peered over the counter.

'Blimey,' whispered a sparrow sitting at the stall. His feathers were matted in tufts around his neck and his black beak curled into a sneering smile. A wiry grey rat with brown, rotting teeth sat beside him. 'Looka that!'

'Have you ever seen anythin' like it?' the rat said under his breath, and nudged the sparrow in the ribs with a bony elbow.

''Allo, Dickin,' the tea seller said. She was a shrew with a long nose and eyes that were magnified behind thick-rimmed glasses partially fogged up with steam. 'What'll it be today?'

'One tea for my little mate, please. Two pinches of sugar.'

The shrew clonked a tarnished thimble on to the counter and Pip's mouth watered, watching a small teapot fill it to the brim. As steam swirled from the thimble, Pip greedily pulled it to her lips.

'Be careful, mate,' Dickin said. 'It's hot!'

Pip ignored him and took a brief sip from the thimble so it would not burn her mouth. The tea felt like a warm hug and as it trickled down her throat, Pip thought of the shop window on the days when the sunshine would pour over the Hanway umbrella and brighten her nest with a cosy glow. For a moment, she could smell Mama as clearly as if she was just over her shoulder and Pip's ears pricked in hope of hearing her and Papa. All too soon, her head caught up with her heart and she let out a long, shuddering sigh that was choked with tears. She pushed the tea thimble away, no longer feeling able to drink it.

'What's wrong, love?' Dickin said. 'Come on, it'll do ya good.'

Pip hung her head and pretended not to hear him.

'Look!' a nearby voice cried in excitement. 'It's Pip!'

'Pip! Is that you?'

She turned to find two familiar faces pushing their way through the crowd. It was Dot and Joe, her friends from the pub next door to James Smith & Sons. Their great-grandparents were once pet mice who had chewed through the bars of their cage and escaped to the cellar. Their family had lived there ever since and Pip had spent many nights with them, exploring underground. One time, they even made it as far as the Shaftesbury Theatre behind the umbrella shop and had watched men and women sing and dance under bright lights on a stage. It had been the most marvellous thing Pip had ever seen.

'Oh, Pip!' Dot squeaked, warmly wrapping her arms around Pip's neck. 'Thank whiskers you're all right! We were so scared something terrible had happened to you and your mama and papa.'

'Have you seen? There's nothing left of your umbrella shop,' Joe said, speaking quickly like he always did when

he was gossiping. 'Or our pub! Mama said if we hadn't been underground we'd be flatter than squashed flies now.'

'Pip,' Dickin said, giving her friends a sniff and standing on all four paws. His kind, brown eyes twinkled with an idea. 'I'm gonna go and find someone that I think can help ya. He's the only one I know that can.' She nodded, moving to follow him, but Dickin shook his head. 'Nah, nah, you stay here with your mates. I know where he is and I'll find him faster if I go on me own. Whatever you do, stay here. I'll be back soon.'

With a warm smile and a wag of his tail that accidentally knocked the roofs off two neighbouring market stalls, he trotted away and quickly vanished into the market crowds.

'Who was that?' Joe said with twitch of his nose. Seeing the tatty red cross stitched to the side of Dickin's white uniform fade into the distance, he let out gasp of excitement. 'Wow! Is he a search and rescue dog? They're heroes! How do you know him? Is he a friend of your mama and papa's? Can I meet him when he gets back?'

'Where *are* your mama and papa?' Dot asked, looking left to right with concern. She laid eyes on the umbrella lying beside the tea stall and smiled with relief. Pip clenched her teeth, sadness threatening to overwhelm her. 'Are they inside the umbrella? Mama will be so happy! We've been keeping an eye out for all of you ever since we arrived yesterday.'

'They're not inside the umbrella!' Pip snapped, with tears stinging her eyes.

'Oh – are they in the market? Our mama keeps going over there to smell the butter and sugar . . .'

'My mama and papa are gone! They're dead!'

As each word left her mouth, Pip felt a throb inside her chest. She turned away from them, biting her lip to stifle the urge to cry. Dot and Joe stared at one another, wide-eyed with shock.

'I'm so sorry, Pip,' Dot said, stepping towards her and sympathetically placing a paw on Pip's shoulder. 'We didn't know.'

'I have an idea!' Joe said, after a long, awkward pause filled with not knowing what to say. He glanced at Dot and smiled. 'Why don't you come and live with us?'

'Yes!' Dot cried. 'It will be so fun! We'll be sisters!'

'And I'll be your brother!'

'We'll be your family, Pip. Our mama and papa will be so pleased!'

Pip paused and smiled uncomfortably. Normally

when Dot and Joe had an idea she believed in it until the end – or at least until they got caught. This time, doubt twisted inside her. She didn't want to go with them.

'Don't worry,' Dot said, rolling her eyes, noticing the look of discomfort on Pip's face. 'You can bring the umbrella.'

Pip looked at it fondly. It belonged with her in the umbrella museum in Gignese where Mama and Papa would want her to be with all the other umbrella mice, not in a bombed-out pub in London. If Mama could make it to Britain inside an umbrella all those years ago then she could make it back to Italy too.

'What's yer story then, ducky?' the rat sitting at the tea stall said, leaning his bony body over the counter and eyeing the young mice with big, gleaming eyes. 'What's yer name?'

'Her name?' Joe said hesitantly, glancing at Dot in mutual surprise at the interruption. Pip recoiled as the rat licked its lips and smiled at her. 'Her name is—'

'Flick,' Pip lied, looking the rat up and down with a scowl.

'Cor!' the sparrow scoffed, jumping off his stool beside the rat and hopping over to Pip on sharp, bony, black talons. 'Don't ya talk proppa! Betcha come from a nice big house.'

'Where I lived was bombed yesterday,' Pip said, firmly wiping away a tear from her whisker and taking a step away from the sparrow with Dot and Joe. Feeling their fur brush hers, she was grateful they were with her now. Standing on her hind paws, she looked over the strangers' shoulders into the crowded market, hoping to see Dickin's scruffy shape padding through the stalls, but he was nowhere to be seen.

'You ain't alone there, ducky,' the rat said, following the sparrow, walking around the umbrella. Reaching out and touching the carved, silver handle, his bony paws lingered on its gold inlay. 'St Giles's fulla them that's been bombed.'

'What ya doin' with that old codger?' asked the sparrow. 'Dickin's good for nothin'.'

'Unless you want an ear full of yap and rubbish,' the rat sneered, arrogantly leaning an elbow on the umbrella handle as if it was his own property. 'Did he tell ya that sob story about "his Jack" and the Blitz?'

'What a load of old codswallop!' The sparrow chuckled.

'We all know he's been with Mr King since day one. He tells that story to everybody he saves so they'll leave their bombed houses and come to St Giles. That way, he gains their trust by makin' them think he's grieving too.'

'Can't put yer faith in a dog, love,' the sparrow said with an earnest shake of his head. 'Everyone knows they're only looking out for themselves.'

'Or their bellies, more like.'

The rat and sparrow sniggered and slapped each other's backs. Pip felt foolish. After all, she didn't know Dickin very well. Nor any dogs for that matter. She remembered Mama and Papa had once explained that dogs were pets because they couldn't remember how to hunt for food. Perhaps it was true he was only helping her so he wouldn't go hungry.

'Listen, missy,' the sparrow said, clearing his throat. 'First things first. There's protocol in St Giles for new arrivals, but you weren't to know. Dickin should've told ya.'

'Protocol?' Pip said.

The mice anxiously looked at one another.

'Yeah, you know,' the rat said, 'forms and that to fill in so you get the right help: A Class when you've lost all yer home. B Class for injured, C Class for orphans, D Class for dead.' The words struck Pip like a blow across her face and she clenched her jaw to stop her lips from trembling. 'There's a big fine if ya don't register.'

'A fine!' Dot and Joe cried.

'Ya might even get a criminal record.'

'Oh dear, mate,' the sparrow said, shaking his head and making a tut-tut sound, 'they won't like it that you've been drinkin' black market tea.'

'Pip!' Dot and Joe gasped, not admitting that they had no idea what black market tea was, having had two cups themselves that morning. 'You'll get into trouble.'

'See, ya can't trust Dickin!' the rat sneered, taking advantage of the look of worry that furrowed Pip's brow. 'He's already gettin' ya in a lot of strife, it's lucky ya found us when ya did.'

'Don't ya worry,' the sparrow said, honourably puffing out his chest feathers. 'We won't say nuffink about your little crimes, including that little fib about your name, eh? That ain't what mates do, is it?' With a gleeful glance at one another, the rat and the sparrow nodded and lifted the umbrella above their heads. 'Come with us, we'll look after ya.'

'No!' Pip said, dashing to the umbrella and standing in front of the bird, trying to block his path. 'I am waiting for Dickin. He'll be back soon.'

'What did we just say about that blinkin' fleabag?' the sparrow said, angrily ruffling the feathers around his neck. 'Dickin ain't coming back for you. You're in St Giles now and he's gone to get his treats like he always does. We're the ones that are really helpin' ya.'

'Yeah,' the rat said, and a crooked smile, filled with long, sharp teeth, spread across his face. 'Don't you know what a favour looks like?'

'What shall we do?' Pip whispered, turning to Dot and Joe and feeling more lost than ever. If she got into trouble here she might never get to Gignese, and without Dickin, she may never get the help she needed to get there.

'I don't know,' Dot said. 'We told Mama we'd be back soon.'

'It won't take a minute, ducky,' the sparrow said, effortlessly stepping around Pip and her friends. Pip gasped in horror as the strangers started to move away from the tea stall with the umbrella carried above their heads. 'You'll see.'

'Stop! I never said you could take my umbrella!'

'Come on,' Joe said, following the rat and sparrow and beckoning Pip and his sister forward with his paw. 'I'm sure it's nothing. Let's get this out of the way, then we can keep exploring. I saw a mouse doing magic tricks earlier. You pick a card from his deck and somehow it ends up behind your ear. You have to see it! It's amazing!'

'Oh!' Dot said, not thinking about her mother any more and giving Pip's paw a tug of encouragement as she trotted to her brother's side. 'I'd love to see that, wouldn't you?'

'I suppose so,' Pip said, and hurried after her friends.

Normally, Dot and Joe's merry banter took her mind off anything, but now she was uneasy. With a last look over her shoulder for a glimpse of Dickin, she sighed with disappointment and walked onward, wondering how she was going to get to Gignese now.

'Make yer life a little brighta!' The sellers' cries grew distant. 'Meat! Butter! Sugar! Get your comforts 'ere!'

CHAPTER SEVEN

THE CROOKS

The umbrella turned many feathered and furry heads as it travelled above the crowd with the young mice trotting after it, trying to keep up with the rat and the sparrow ahead of them. Leaving the safety of the market far behind, the nervous flutter in Pip's chest quickly grew to a drumming thud of dread as they reached a dark corner where no other creature roamed.

'You're talking absolute rubbish!' Dot scoffed, gleefully bickering with her little brother. 'You couldn't even pull off a magic trick to fool a blind mouse!'

'I could!' Joe scowled with his fur standing on end.

'Not even a deaf, dumb *and* blind mouse!'

'All right then. When we get back, I'll show you!'

'I bet you can't.'

'I bet I can.'

'I bet you can't!'

'I bet I can!'

'What do you think, Pip? Wouldn't he be the worst magician in the world?'

Pip's ears cocked on her head but she wasn't listening. The rat and the sparrow were leading them and the umbrella towards a small shadowy opening in a brick wall, similar to the one she and Dickin had used to enter St Giles. But this one had green moss and black slime glistening around its edges and the sound of water trickling nearby.

'Stop!' Pip said firmly, hurrying ahead of Dot and Joe so she was walking briskly alongside the strangers. 'Where are you taking us and my umbrella?'

'It's not far, mate,' the rat said nonchalantly without turning his head. He quickened his pace along with the sparrow. 'Just around this corner and we'll settle everything. Don'tcha worry. Everybody does it when they arrive.'

'Don't be such a worry-guts,' Joe said. 'The sooner we get this over and done with, the sooner we'll get back to the market.'

'I suggest you lot hurry up,' the sparrow said loudly. 'It gets busy up there when them bombs come crashin'.'

The strangers scuttled forward and vanished through the opening in the wall. The young mice broke into a run behind them and swiftly climbed through into an enormous underground sewer canal. It smelt of musty laundry and was enveloped by a gloomy domed brick tunnel. A wide expanse of black water with no beginning and no end rushed below the narrow ledge they found themselves on. The umbrella was dropped to the ground, where it smacked against the concrete. The clatter echoed along the tunnel, as if the bricks were laughing at them.

'First things first,' the sparrow said, turning to loom over Pip with its sharp, ebony beak glinting in the gloom. 'You owe us arrival and insurance tax.'

'What?' Pip said, staring fearfully at the umbrella lying so close to the water.

68

'Every bein' pays it,' the rat said with a sneer. The mice looked nervously at his long yellow teeth and drew closer to each other. 'It's the law in St Giles.'

'But we don't have any money.'

'Prove it!'

The mice glanced at one another nervously and innocently held out their empty paws. Shaking their heads with disapproval, the strangers tut-tutted and stepped towards them with a jeering snarl.

'They'll lock you up and throw away the key!'

'You'll never see the light of day again.'

The mice stepped backwards, looking desperately over their shoulders for a place to run, but the rat and sparrow encircled them, licking their lips like wolves, pacing around their prey.

'Your punishment is simple: your umbrella is forfeit,' the rat said with a menacing smile. His eyes pored over the umbrella's silver handle and its gold inlay carvings, both flickering in the gloom. 'Now scram, you pesky little varmints,' he said, snarling at the mice, 'or we'll rip ya into little pieces.'

'No,' Pip snapped, defiantly scowling into the rat's empty black eyes. But inside, she felt more frightened than ever and she held her arms tightly by her sides to control her trembling limbs. She was an umbrella mouse and she wasn't letting anyone take her home, her history and her last piece of Mama and Papa. It was all she had left.

Dot and Joe shivered with fear beside her and began carefully edging away from the rat and sparrow, who were baring their teeth at Pip like wild animals about to pounce on their prey.

'What did you just say?' the sparrow said, feathers ruffling furiously all over its body.

'Careful, mate,' the rat growled. 'St Giles can be a very dangerous place, especially for little 'uns.'

Pip stood on her tiptoes and glared into the sparrow's cold, black eyes.

'I said – NO!'

Instantly, the rat snapped its claws around her neck and lifted her off the ground. Seeing their chance for escape, Joe snatched Dot's paw in his and they bolted back towards the market, vanishing in the gloom like spectres into shadows. Gasping desperately for air, Pip thrashed wildly in the rat's grasp and managed to free herself. She dropped to the ground on all fours, breathless, and dashed to the umbrella at once. She guarded it, feeling the fur along her spine bristle with terror and fury.

'You wriggly little blighter!' the rat said in astonishment.

'Look at her!' the sparrow sniggered. 'Do you really think a little mouse like you can stop us taking what we want?'

'I'll never let you take my umbrella away from me!' Pip growled. 'You stay away from us!'

'We'll see about that!' the rat said, stalking forward beside the sparrow and curling its lips around its long yellow teeth in a snarl. Holding her breath, Pip clenched her paws into fists.

It was then that a great flash of fur burst headlong into the fray. A fearful growl sounded, the sounds of a scuffle, then a splash, closely followed by a second. Pip watched the rat and sparrow caught in the swirl of the water, desperately scrapping with one another as they struggled to keep their heads above the fetid surface. Gasping, they bobbed and ducked under, the inky black water swallowing them whole. Suddenly the tunnel was quiet, save for the sounds of the underground river flowing into the gloom.

'Are you all right?' Dickin asked, rushing to Pip and affectionately touching his furry forehead to her own with relief.

'Yes,' Pip said, wobbling to her hind paws, trying to ignore the fear still pulsing through her little body. 'I think I'm OK.'

'You ninny!' he growled, gently cuffing the back of her ears. Wincing, she hung her head in shame. 'Where are yer mates? I told ya to stay with them and *not* leave the tea stall. You're lucky those crooks didn't skin ya alive!'

'What friends? They ran away to save their own skins, just like they've done before! And what was I supposed to do?' she snapped. She felt stupid enough without Dickin telling her off. 'That rat and sparrow told me you lied about Mr King and your Jack to get me to come to St Giles.'

'What?' Dickin said, his ears drooping on his head.

'They said I was in trouble for not signing a form telling them I was an orphan and I'd have to pay a fine. They told me that you weren't coming back for me and that they were going to help me instead.' She paused, feeling her chest swell with anger. 'How was I supposed to know they were going to trick me? I don't know this place and I don't know you! How do I know you won't try to hurt me too? Or steal the umbrella as well! Or run away to save your own skin! I never should have come here with you.'

'Shhh, Pip,' he said softly, sitting on his haunches and drawing her close to him with his paw. She buried her face in his soft belly fur and whimpered. 'It's all right, love, you're safe now. There are real friends in this world and then there are those that hurt ya after they seemed to be on yer side. They're there to teach us who to trust and when to stand alone and it ain't ever an easy lesson to learn. But I promise ya, I'm yer mate. I always will be and I'm sorry, I never should have left ya like I did.'

At that moment, Pip's insides leaped with surprise, as she felt a warm, bony paw rest heavily on her shoulder.

'Worry not, little one,' said a voice that she knew was not from Britain. 'Without mistakes, your life will never know adventure.'

Comforted by his words, she looked up to meet his gaze, but at once she turned her eyes away with a shiver. The rat was tall and lean with rich, dark fur. His ears were scratched to ribbons and jagged scars were torn across his face and body.

'Pip, this is Hans,' Dickin said, reading the fear in Pip's eyes. 'He's German but you can trust him. He's on our side and he's fought bravely for the Allied cause.'

'Introductions can wait,' Hans said, his eyes gleaming

in the shadows. 'Where there's one crook there are many and I don't intend to be here when they come scavenging for a fight.'

'Climb up, Pip,' Dickin said, standing on four paws and dipping his head to the ground with a wag of his tail. 'And make sure you get a good hold.'

She clutched the dog's fur in both front paws and clambered to Dickin's collar, taking a firm grip of his wiry, black coat behind his neck. Hans followed, agilely climbing up beside her. Pip shied away, feeling a prickly uneasiness being so close to him, but what happened next made her forget he even existed.

Dickin picked up the umbrella in his teeth and cast it into the rushing black water.

BERNARD BOOTH

Dickin sprang after the umbrella, soaring though the air and plunging into the cold underground canal. Instantly the current carried them through the gloom. Panting with effort, Dickin caught the umbrella between his teeth and began awkwardly paddling across the rushing water.

'You didn't think I'd chuck this beauty away, did ya?' he said, his muffled voice echoing off the walls. Pip breathed a sigh of relief.

A few minutes brought them to a junction where the tunnel split, going in two directions. To the right, the water increased in speed, gushing downwards into the shadows. Feeling it tug at his paws, Dickin swam hard to the left. Treading water for a moment at the point of no return, he struggled out of its grasp and entered a brick tunnel off to the left. The water quickly grew calm and soon he no longer needed to swim. Wading through the murky water, they arrived in a large, square chamber with a domed ceiling and a pair of enormous rusty doors fixed to the furthest wall. Dragging his dripping wet body on to two stone steps above the water, Dickin gently dropped the umbrella at the foot of the doors as Pip and Hans dismounted beside him.

'What is this place?' Pip said, staring wide-eyed at the chamber.

'This is a part of the ancient River Fleet,' Dickin said. 'It runs from Hampstead in North London and flows south, underground, until it reaches the River Thames.'

'Why did I never know it was here?'

'Not many do since London was built over it and it was turned into a sewer, but it ain't all bad that it's been forgotten. You'll see.'

The rat stepped forward and thumped the door with a loud, hollow clang. A moment later, a tiny peephole slid open.

'Who's there?' a deep voice boomed from the other side of the door. A solitary eye stared through the hole, suspiciously flicking between Pip, Dickin and Hans. 'State your name and purpose.'

'It's Hans,' the rat said, rolling his eyes with an impatient sigh. 'We have come with a friend to see Bernard Booth.'

The peephole snapped shut. A click followed, then a long groan as the huge door opened just enough for Dickin, Pip, Hans and the umbrella carried above their heads to step inside. Astonished, Pip saw the porter was not a giant creature at all, but a tiny field mouse looking through the peephole by means of a ladder, his booming voice having come from a long, black speaking trumpet he held by his side. The field mouse jumped to a rope hanging nearby and slowly slid down it to the ground. A moment later, water cascaded over a vast timber wheel that stood against the inner wall. As it turned, the enormous door closed with a deep, metallic thud.

'Good evening,' the tiny field mouse said with great authority, especially for one so small. 'Bernard is in his office. You know where to go.'

Still sopping wet, Dickin gave Pip a nudge with his nose.

'Watch this.'

The dog stood next to the field mouse and gleefully shook himself from head to tail.

'Dickin! You rotten mongrel!' squealed the field mouse. His sodden fur hung from his skinny little body and obscured his eyes, making his ears look as big as balloons on top of his head. Pip giggled for the first time since the bomb had hit. It felt strange and unfamiliar, as if she was laughing inside a different body.

'That never gets old!' Dickin laughed, triumphantly trotting forward with his head held high and his tail wagging from side to side.

Ahead was the strangest room Pip had ever seen. Electric Christmas lights were again hung from the arched ceiling and brick walls, but it was the hub of activity they illuminated on the concrete floor below that amazed her. The huge square room was divided into quarters, each part using a section of wall. In the front half, a map of the world covered with pins dominated the space to the left and rows of desks made up the section to the right. A mixture of mice, rats, blackbirds, robins, sparrows and blue tits sat at the desks, intensely focusing on scribbling notes while wearing little black headphones and pressing little rectangular triggers, making strange *ditt*ing and *dahh*ing sounds.

An albino rat moved about them collecting their papers before briskly walking to the rear half of the room. A map of Europe was fixed above a large table, where twelve more small animals sat on chairs made from matchboxes. As the white rat delivered the messages and returned to the other side of the room, the animals at the large table pored over the notes with their brows furrowed in thought. Next to this section was a tall metal house with 'BREAD' printed on its outside wall, and smoke trickled from a chimney that had the word 'SPAM' just visible under a layer of soot. Behind it stood a row of four blue and brown smaller houses, each with a pigeon roosting inside and 'HUNTLEY & PALMER'S BREAKFAST BISCUITS' written in blue on each wall.

As Pip, Dickin and Hans approached, only one animal looked up. Standing between the metal house and the animals working feverishly under the map of Europe, an elderly pigeon with pale grey feathers, a round purple belly and a double chin lowered a document from his gaze and quizzically cocked his head in their direction. Tapping the ground with his walking stick, he tottered towards them, tucking the papers under his wing.

'Good afternoon, Dickin, Hans.' He smiled, pushing his horn-rimmed spectacles up his beak as he watched the rat and Pip lower the umbrella to the ground. 'Gosh. Who have we here?'

'This is Pip Hanway,' Dickin said, sitting down. 'She needs your help, sir. We've just come from St Giles.'

'Well, I will help as best I can,' the pigeon said, hobbling towards her. He took her little paw in his wing and firmly shook it. Pip stared into his intelligent amber eyes and quickly looked away. The bird had an air of wisdom and authority that made her nervous. 'I am Bernard Booth. Sit, rest – you're looking awfully peaky, I must say. Don't be shy. Here –' he walked over to the house and pulled a white dice with black spots from under a small table on the porch – 'sit.'

'Thank you,' Pip said timidly, and wearily clambered on to the dice. Dickin sat on the ground next to her, while Hans slumped on to an old cotton reel on her other side with a sigh of relaxation and stretched his legs out before him.

Pip looked around the room with growing curiosity. Seeing the animals frown and stick the tips of their tongues out of the corners of their mouths in concentration, she was sure the strange '*dit-dit-dit-dah*' sounds punctuating the silence meant something very important. So must the multicoloured pins dotted all over the two maps. She longed to have a closer look but at that moment, a rattle turned her head. Standing in the doorway to his metal house, clutching the doorframe with one wing, Bernard held a tray with a china teapot, cups and saucers, and a dish with a lid that did not match. A glorious, sweet smell wafted from it.

'Lucky for you . . .' Bernard cooed with a wobble. At once the rat jumped from his stool, took the tray from him and placed it gently on the table. The pigeon's joints creaked with effort as he hobbled towards them, leaning on his walking stick. When comfortably seated between Pip and Hans, he lifted the lid of the dish. 'You're just in time for afternoon tea.'

'Victoria sponge!' cried Pip with a broad smile that popped her whiskers upright on her cheeks. 'We only have cake at Christmas!'

'Like so many of us – wartime rationing makes cake a rare sight for us all,' Bernard cooed, pouring tea into a cup and handing it to her. 'As you would have seen, St Giles is the gathering ground for every creature in trouble, no matter where they are from. But sadly, desperate times attract crooks and thieves, who profit from stolen goods and black market trading – selling snatched rations at ridiculously unfair prices. But here we're not far from the Savoy Hotel and they have marvellous food in their cupboards – *unrationed* tea, sugar, meat and wine – that they sell to legally paying customers, so if we're careful and have a little bit of luck, we get some good scraps from time to time.' He took a bite of the cake and sighed with contentment. 'And when the world seems mad, sometimes it takes just one simple pleasure for it to make sense again. Eat, eat!'

The cake melted in their mouths. Every bite took Pip far away from where she was, where she had been that day and where she had to go. For the first time, she felt a twinge of excitement for the journey ahead. Mama and Papa would have been pleased she was going to find her mother's family at the umbrella museum. But thinking of them immediately brought tears to her eyes and she fiercely wished they were with her, eating cake and getting ready to go to Gignese too.

'How can this be happening?' she said, ignoring her last bite of sponge and feeling a hot anger rising inside her. 'I thought we were winning the war now America has joined us and the Soviet Union as allies. Everyone who came into the shop was saying after we stormed the Normandy beaches on D-Day that the war could be over soon. But now it feels like the bombs are falling more than ever and nobody is safe.' The fur along her spine bristled with furious sorrow. 'I don't understand.'

'These new V-1 rockets are Hitler's vengeance weapons,' Dickin said. 'Now that we have a foothold in

France, the Allies have a chance of crossing the continent and closin' in on Germany and he's as mad as a hatter about it.'

'The lull is over, my friends,' Bernard cooed seriously after a sip of tea. 'And sadly I believe it will become worse before it gets better. We must be more vigilant than ever.'

'D-Day has paved the way,' Dickin said, seeing Pip's ears flatten anxiously on her head. 'The Allies will succeed, you'll see – so don'tcha worry a whisker, love. We've got a hell of a lot of good souls on our team fightin' and resisting the enemy in countries all over the world. With their help and a bit of time, we'll end this stinkin' war.'

'But how do you know that?' Pip said. 'Who knows who's going to win the war now?'

'Because we will never tire in our quest for victory,' Bernard said firmly, sitting tall with his chest feathers plumping confidently. 'As Churchill says, we shall have victory in spite of all terror, however long and hard the road may be. For without victory there is no survival, young Pip.' His wise orange eyes stared deeply into hers. 'Each of us must strive without failing in faith or in duty. Only then will the dark curse of war be lifted from our age.'

'Both humans and animals are battlin' on the frontlines but we're fightin' on home soil too, mate,' Dickin said, and his eyes gleamed with pride. 'All day and all night right under your nose. Listen.'

'What *is* that?' Pip said, hearing the *dit-dit-dah* noises in the room.

'It's Morse code,' said Bernard. 'We're delivering secret messages to the human and animal French Resistance by sending different pulses of electric current they then pick up on hidden crystal radios throughout France. Each combination of *dit-dah* and the silence between them represents a number or a letter of the alphabet. Each message they receive gives instructions on how to weaken enemy power.'

'And what do the messages say?' Pip asked, riveted to his every word.

'Many secret things – sometimes they give instructions to sabotage electrical equipment or transport lines by road or rail so the enemy can't use them for advancing forward or for carrying food or weapons. Other times they give locations to rescue another fighter or deliver supplies to those that need them nearby.'

'So what you're talking about are spy missions?' Pip said excitedly, sitting bolt upright, remembering the man wearing the fedora hat who had come into the shop and asked Mr Smith to make him the secret weapon umbrellas. 'For Churchill's Secret Army?'

'Or in our case – Churchill's Secret *Animal* Army.' Bernard smiled. 'Since the first wars were fought among men, animals have been secretly helping war efforts in ways humans would never believe, even if they saw it with their own eyes. After all, the world is as much ours as it is theirs. But the humans don't know we're doing it, which puts the "Secret" into Churchill's Secret Animal Army,' Bernard said. 'As with all wars, there are two sides. We are helping the Allied forces while the Axis animals fight to preserve Hitler's rule. And our network spreads far and wide, young Pip. From ordinary mice eavesdropping on human spies in hotel rooms, to the bravest dogs sniffing for mines alongside men in combat. And let us not forget our friends like Dickin here, rescuing people and animals from bomb blasts with his nose.' The terrier gave Pip a wink. 'Furthermore, there's Hans – a German rat who has risked his life resisting the Nazis on his home soil.'

'I did what was necessary,' the rat insisted, his scarred jaw hardening with difficult memories. 'I could not watch my country be crushed under Hitler's jackboot.'

'Hans's knowledge of German customs and his ability to translate intercepted messages from the enemy have made him one of our most valuable members,' Bernard cooed, and the rat shifted uncomfortably on his cotton reel. 'Learn how to take a compliment, old chap!' the pigeon said, slapping him on the back with his wing. 'Courage is the finest quality because it guarantees all other virtues. Hans bravely escaped the enemy after they had nearly torn him to pieces and crossed the border into France before stowing away on a Lysander plane collecting humans from the French Resistance, all so he could join our fight here in Britain.'

Hans gave a slow, humble nod to the pigeon in thanks and Pip shuddered, eyeing the marks of violence scored across body.

'Morse code is the fastest way for us to deliver and receive information from both our animal and human connections,' Bernard cooed, and a smile drew across his beak. 'But what really makes me chuckle is that our human contacts have no idea they are sometimes communicating with animals.'

'And they think *we're* the ignorant beasts,' Hans scoffed.

'Exactly! They'd never believe it! Nor would they

suspect their own messenger pigeons.' He gestured with his wing to the smaller structures behind his house. Turning to look over her shoulder, Pip's eyes shone with curiosity as she saw pigeons peacefully roosting in their coops. 'The fastest of us can fly a mile a minute. Well –' Bernard smiled self-consciously, tapping his walking stick on the ground – 'once upon a time, in my case.'

'So you use pigeons for sending secret messages as well as Morse code?' Pip asked, turning back to the elderly bird.

'That's right. The birds are more mobile and don't rely on electricity,' Bernard continued. 'But it's a risky business. On every errand, they can be shot or injured by shrapnel. Axis falcons hunt the skies for them too, and few survive the chase these days.'

'What do the messages say?'

'That's top secret information, young Pip!' he cooed, touching the side of his beak twice with the tip of his wing. 'And as our motto states: *A secret is only a secret if it remains unspoken.* Although I can tell you they give instructions and share knowledge about enemy and Allied movements and so on, just like Morse code.'

'But if these war pigeons are fighting with the humans, how can they work for Churchill's Secret

Animal Army at the same time?'

'Every time they complete a human mission, they are given leave to rest in their home coop and when they are released for exercise, they slip away to volunteer for us. Let me introduce them to you,' Bernard said, proudly pointing his wing to each coop housing a roosting pigeon. 'That's the Duke of Normandy, the first pigeon to arrive back in Britain from enemy lines during the D-Day invasion. And that's GI Joe – he's our swiftest bird, who saved over a hundred Allied soldiers and many more Italian civilians from an airstrike when radios failed. Alongside him is Blackie Harrington, you see the scars across his chest and neck?'

Pip nodded, her ears pricked up high.

'He delivered a key message even after he was bloody with shrapnel wounds. And if you think that's impressive,' Bernard continued, pointing to a smaller pigeon with neat white markings around her eyes, 'Mary of Exeter is unstoppable. She has been blown up, shot, attacked by a falcon *and* hit by shrapnel. She's had twenty-two stitches, that's the equivalent of four thousand stitches in a human soldier, although I doubt a man could survive to tell the tale.

'Now you know all about us,' Bernard said, turning

to the little mouse still gazing at the pigeons. 'Tell me – why do you need my help, young Pip?'

Fighting the tears filling her eyes, Pip recounted the hours that had led her to Bernard Booth's door since the bomb hit James Smith & Sons Umbrellas. Cooing thoughtfully, the pigeon listened with his head sympathetically cocked to one side.

'If you were alone and if everything you knew had been taken away from you,' Pip finished with a sniff, 'wouldn't you try to find the last souls that loved you?'

There was silence. Her words struck Bernard, Hans and Dickin in such a way that none immediately had the heart to deny her impossible quest. Each had lost their homes and families in the war too, and none would ever fully recover from such sorrow. At last, Bernard spoke.

'Pip,' he said, cooing gravely, 'this journey holds no hope. Mainland Europe is still very much at war, even after our victories in Normandy and southern Italy. Crossing the English Channel to northern France is fraught with danger from beginning to end. Even if you make it, the enemy occupy the rest of France and northern Italy and if they catch you, you may meet a fate worse than death.' He shook his head. 'I fear you will not make it.'

'But my mother made it to England from Italy inside an umbrella – I know I can too. I have to try.'

'Try as you might, this is not the time to travel to Italy and we cannot simply deliver you there like a postman. Your duty is to your country and we all have to pull together if we are going to win this war.' He sighed. 'I'm sorry, but I cannot help you.'

'I will do whatever it takes!' Pip cried. 'Please let me go!'

'I will help her,' Hans said, looking at Bernard with a keen determination. 'I have waited for my chance to return to my homeland for three years. With the Allies advancing upon Germany, I can gather vital information to open the path and send it back to you here. They say that with the help of the Americans and the Soviets, the war will not last much longer and I belong in Bavaria by Lake Eibsee, where my clan has lived and died for longer than memory. I wish to spend the rest of my days in a free Fatherland. I will deliver Pip to Gignese, then I will make my own way to Germany and help you bring an end to this war from there.'

'No,' Bernard said firmly, his neck feathers ruffling impatiently around his neck. 'It makes no sense for you to join a suicide mission when your duty is to the Allied cause. The war is not over yet.' He abruptly stood from the table and began hobbling back to his house, shaking his head. 'Not by a long shot, and you know more than any of us what we are fighting against. Dickin, please take Pip back to her friends in St Giles. She needs food and plenty of rest after everything she has been through.'

'Please,' Pip said desperately, leaping from her seat. 'They're not my friends, didn't you hear me? They left me to be skinned alive by those thieves! I never want to see them again.'

'Now, now, Pip,' the terrier said calmly, glancing at Hans brooding with frustration at the table. 'There's no point fightin' over this. You're better off this way. And Bernard's right – it's time you caught up with some shut-eye. You ain't slept a wink and you've had a nasty shock.' He tenderly nudged her with his shiny black nose. 'Come on, let's get ya back to yer mates.'

'The humans need our help more than ever, young Pip,' Bernard cooed from his doorway. 'As you say, we've taken Normandy back but it's a long, hard, road to Berlin. We must all make sacrifices and above all we must be brave,' he said with a kind smile. 'It has been a pleasure to meet you. Good luck, and remember you must never give in. *Never*, except to the convictions of honour, courage and good sense.' The pigeon turned his attention to Dickin and pointed his wing beyond the dozing pigeons. 'You may take her via the river footpath and save yourself the swim. Hans, come inside – we have much to discuss.'

Despair thumped in Pip's chest as she watched the rat and pigeon step into Bernard's house and close the door as if she had never existed. Once again, Dickin took the umbrella between his teeth and beckoned her with a wagging tail to climb to the back of his neck. She shook her head and scowled.

'Have it your way,' he said, slowly padding past the roosting pigeons towards a dark corridor that led to the underground river footpath. 'You'll cheer up once you've had some grub and a kip.'

Ignoring him, Pip stepped to Bernard's door and pressed her ear against it, hoping to hear him and Hans mention anything about her plan. But as she stepped closer she heard something else entirely.

'You and GI Joe shall conduct Operation Popeye with a group of French Resistance animals in Normandy called Noah's Ark. The Axis animals will do anything to stop you so you must be on your guard. If this mission succeeds, we will be one step closer to stopping Hitler.

When you and GI Joe deliver the message . . .'

Before Pip heard more, Dickin looked over his shoulder and uttered a low, insistent growl.

'I mean it, mate.' He barked gruffly, marching towards her with the umbrella in his mouth. 'If Bernard catches you eavesdroppin' you'll be in a ton of trouble. Come with me now.'

He turned and continued walking away, trusting Pip to follow. Flicking her tail in frustration, she reluctantly moved away from Bernard's door, racking her brain for anything she could do to make him change his mind. It was then that her eyes caught sight of a small, tightly rolled-up scroll of paper next to one of the sleeping pigeons. It was GI Joe, and at once her mind leaped with an idea. With a quick glance around her, she dashed for it, tucked it under her arm and hurried to Dickin with her heart thundering inside her ears.

'That's it,' he said, feeling her scurry up his front leg to the back of his neck, 'I knew you'd come round.'

Pip smiled. Somehow, as soon as she found a way, she and the umbrella would leave for France and deliver the message to the French Resistance in exchange for safe passage to Gignese.

CHAPTER NINE

THE RIVER THAMES

Pip flinched every time the paper scroll crinkled under her arm as Dickin returned to the dark underground canal tunnel, following a stone footpath that ran alongside the black, rushing water. With each step the river grew louder and as it swelled to a roar, she watched it race downwards and shoot through a large opening in a wall that brought the tunnel to an end.

'Not far now,' Dickin said, rounding a corner to the right and stepping into a side tunnel thick with shadows. 'I'll find us a nice sarnie when we get back to St Giles. And I bet your mates will be happy to see ya after everythin' that's happened to ya.'

'They don't give a stuff about me,' Pip said, remembering the altercation with the thieves. 'If they did, they never would have left me like that. I don't need them or their stinking friendship. I don't need anybody.'

'It sounds like you've got a lonely life ahead of you then. Everybody needs somebody.'

Pip's throat tightened. She already knew she had a lonely life ahead of her without Mama and Papa. She closed her eyes and pictured Mama's kind face that righted every wrong, and Papa's smile that was as warm as it was mischievous. She wondered what they would do if they were with her now as she took the scroll from under her arm. Slowly and carefully, keeping an eye on Dickin's twitching ears, she unpeeled the edge of the roll of paper to see what was inside.

At that moment, a dark figure darted across their path, closely followed by a second. Coming to an abrupt stop, Dickin squinted in the gloom with a vigorous sniff. Quickly hiding the scroll under her arm again, Pip's nose twitched uneasily, smelling something that made her shudder.

'Who's there?' Dickin growled, the fur on the back of his neck bristling with unease. 'Answer me!' he yapped. 'Now!'

'Well look who it is.' A sharp voice sneered in the darkness, speaking loudly over the river rushing nearby.

A growl rumbled in Dickin's throat as he took two cautious steps backwards to the water's edge.

'Twice in one day,' another voice said, revealing sharp, rotting teeth in the gloom. 'Now there's a stroke a luck!'

Watching the figures step closer, Pip gasped with horror. It was the crooks, and both bore crimson cuts from the fight with Hans and Dickin earlier that day. The rat's ears were torn to ribbons and the sparrow could only open one eye.

'Climb down and stay back, Pip,' the terrier said urgently, dipping his head to the ground. Pip clambered down at once and dashed to a nearby wall, holding the scroll tighter than ever under her arm. 'This could get ugly.'

'You bet it will, fleabag,' the sparrow snarled. 'I've thought of nuffin' else since you chucked us in the canal.'

Dickin growled, curling his lips around his sharp white fangs. At once, the thieves pounced on his muzzle and the dog yelped as claws, teeth and talons ripped into his fur. With a frenzied shake of his head, the umbrella struck their bodies and hurled them away from him. At the same moment, Dickin gasped as it slipped from his jaws and slammed into the wall above Pip with a bang.

Diving out of harm's way, she cried out with fear as the umbrella bounced off the bricks and fell dangerously close to the edge of the side tunnel, and the water rushing through the opening below.

The rat leaped to the umbrella as the sparrow clawed and pecked at Dickin's eyes and nose. Before the rat could snatch the canopy, Pip threw herself to the umbrella's silver handle, perilously hanging over the water's edge, and hurried along it with her heart in her throat. Remembering Papa teaching her about Jonas Hanway and the King of Persia, she pressed the small button concealed in a carved fig leaf on its side, bursting the canopy open. Catapulted into the air, the rat hurled into the sparrow, knocking him from his vicious perch on Dickin's head. As the crooks tumbled to the ground, the dog pounced with a fearful roar. Scrapping together in a ball of fur and feathers, two crunches sounded as Dickin's jaws snapped shut around them.

Breathless with horror, Pip turned away and looked at the water below, rushing through the large hole in the wall. Beyond it, there was a glimmer of sunlight shimmering on the surface of a great expanse of water moving swiftly to the left. Her whiskers popped upright with an idea. Dickin had told her the River Fleet ended when it flowed into the River Thames. Mama and Papa had taught her the Thames was the only big river in London, flowing into the North Sea, which led to mainland Europe. Her heart raced with a sudden impulse. She had the message in the scroll – if she could sail the umbrella to Normandy she'd have her chance to help the French Resistance in exchange for help in getting to Italy. This was it!

With a glance at Dickin, who was still a few paces away from her, she ran up inside the open umbrella canopy and pushing it with all her might, she turned it around to face the canal.

'What are you doing?' the dog yapped urgently, hearing the umbrella scrape roughly across the ground. As he hurried to reach the umbrella, it tipped over the edge and hit the swiftly moving water below with a small splash. 'No!' he howled, shifting nervously on his paws as he considered jumping in after her. 'That's the Thames! The water is too dangerous! Humans drown in there!'

'I'll be all right!' Pip cried.

The truth was that she had no idea what was going to happen now. All she knew was that she had to get herself and the umbrella to Gignese – she couldn't stay in St Giles with all its bad friends and thieves. And if Dickin, Hans and Bernard Booth couldn't help her, then she had to help herself.

As she looked up at the terrier desperately sprinting alongside the rushing water, tears filled her eyes. She was really going to miss him. He had been the best friend she had ever had.

'No!' Dickin barked desperately, seeing the scroll under Pip's arm. 'That's not meant for you! You'll never make it!'

'Goodbye, Dickin!' Pip said. 'Thank you for—'

But before she could say more, the water gurgled and the umbrella abruptly slammed onto its side as it was sucked through the opening. Plunging downwards, it smacked the surface of the Thames and span in a circle. Lying flat on her back against the canopy, Pip stared into the enormous, swirling clouds glowing with the first pinks and oranges of sunset. As the strong current swiftly carried the umbrella across the water, her ears pricked as she heard a familiar melody. Carefully scampering to the top of the upturned silver handle, she looked upstream. In the increasing distance, towering over the enormous river and the surrounding buildings, stood a long, slim, silhouette pointing into a coral sky. As its bells tolled eight o'clock, she saw Big Ben for the first time.

Soon, the dappled clouds above the Thames bled scarlet and violet, and in the fading light London laid

bare its wounds from the past five years of war. Each destroyed building stood for another devastated family, and Pip's heart grew heavy wondering how the world had become so mad with war and hatred. The great, unharmed grey dome of St Paul's Cathedral passed by and at once she felt stronger for seeing it standing tall above the ruins. Whatever happened in France, she couldn't fail, because she would have tried. *Mama and Papa would be proud of that*, she thought, unravelling the scroll in her paws to look inside.

"'John has a long moustache,'" she read aloud. It sounded ridiculous and made no sense to her at all.

Knowing she was finally on her way to Italy, the weight of the previous day and night clung to every hair on her body. Weak with exhaustion, she carefully clambered down the umbrella handle to the canopy, carrying the scroll in her paw, and crawled behind the top notch where her family nest used to be. With a yawn that shuddered her body from the tips of her whiskers to the end of her tail, she curled into a little ball and fell into a deep, dreamless sleep.

But as Pip gently rocked back and forth inside the umbrella bobbing across the water, a shuddering boom sounded in the distance downstream.

CHAPTER TEN

THE VOYAGE

The air grew dense with thunder, and dark, anvil-shaped clouds flashed with lightning as the umbrella snaked along the River Thames. As night set in, the buildings along the riverbank thinned, until they were replaced by fields of sun-scorched grass swishing in the gloom above muddy-brown waters rippling along the marshland. Further ahead, the river expanded into a vast blanket of water, like an enormous, wet slate floor, white crests of waves somersaulting across its surface. Above it, the sky blackened in an inhospitable temper, as if displeased that the umbrella had entered its house uninvited, blowing a forbidding wind in its direction.

Pip woke with a start, feeling the umbrella bump and sway on the choppy waters beneath her. Groggily lifting her head and opening her eyes, for a brief moment she thought she was at home in the umbrella shop. But as she shivered against the cold, she quickly realized she was alone, and a long shuddering sigh escaped her lips as she remembered the horror and sadness of the day before.

A chilly midnight air blustered about her fur as she clambered up to the umbrella handle and stared into the gloom behind her. Pip had drifted far from the riverbanks of London and into the Thames Estuary. Turning to face the waves merging into the North Sea beyond, she was astonished to see a group of curious metal houses standing out of the water on stilts. Each had two floors and a row of glass windows, and a bridge connecting it to its neighbour. Huge, long-barrelled guns pointed into the sky from every roof. Pip's ears flattened, hearing a mechanic rattle approaching high above. Her heart shivered as it grew louder and suddenly the guns screamed to life in a blaze of light, firing into the night sky and making the air shudder. A pointed black plane with stumpy wings and a thick tail dropped through the clouds, smashing into the sea. A tower of white water soared into the air and the umbrella surged up and down in a sickening sway.

A strange clattering sounded above her as strong,

beating wings and curved black claws dived through the sky towards her. Lurching backwards out of harm's way, Pip's heart clamoured in her ears as she felt the empty air close around her, pulling her towards the choppy waters below.

'Don't worry liddle lady,' a deep, velvety voice cooed in an American accent. At the same moment, bony claws snapped around her wrist and yanked her upwards to the handle. 'We gotcha!'

Thunder rumbled. Before her, Hans straddled the back of a broad-chested pigeon with a white stripe across his beak.

'How did you find me?' Pip said, scowling with annoyance.

'Dickin went straight to Bernard Booth when you ran away,' Hans said and a smile drew across his scarred face. 'You've got guts doing what you did.'

'Guts!' The pigeon laughed as the rat dismounted, carrying a pouch made from a tied-up red and white polka dot handkerchief. Unravelling it, he expertly rigged it to the umbrella handle with string. 'Crazy-assed stubbornness, I'd say. Nobody has ever backed Bernard Booth into a corner like you have. He's sent us to make sure that message gets to where it needs to go and now we've got no choice but to take you with us.' He cocked his head at the scroll tightly clasped in Pip's paw. 'I believe you have something that belongs to me, miss.'

'No,' she said, drawing the paper close to her chest. '*I'm* delivering it to the French Resistance.'

A crash of thunder boomed above, making each of them cower in alarm. Fat raindrops pitter-pattered about them, drenching their fur and feathers.

'This is GI Joe,' Hans said, shouting over the howling wind. 'He's the fastest pigeon we have and that message must get to Noah's Ark in Normandy by midday tomorrow.'

'But I need it!' Pip said desperately. 'It's all I have to help me get to Italy.'

'If you don't give GI Joe the scroll, we'll miss our chance!' Hans said, gravely staring into her eyes. 'The message is worthless if it doesn't get to the Resistance in time and you don't know where you are going.' The rat clenched his jaw with impatience. 'Pip, you have no idea what you're doing. You are drifting on open seas!'

Hans's words hit Pip's pride like a blow to the face. He was right – she didn't know which way she was sailing or how she would locate the Resistance in

Normandy. Nor had she thought how long it would take to find them. She didn't think it would matter, she just needed to get to France and then she'd look for them.

'And if the message gets into the wrong hands, you waste all the work we've done!' He held out his paw for the scroll. 'Give it to me now, Pip. Lives are at risk.'

'Fine!' she frowned, slamming the scroll into Hans's open paw with shame burning inside her. 'I'm sorry, I didn't know!'

'Believe me,' GI Joe cooed as Hans urgently inserted the scroll into a small canister attached to the bird's ankle, 'this message will pave your way to Italy.' He glanced at Hans and his amber eyes glowed with determination. 'See you on the other side.'

With a robust flap of his wings, GI Joe soared upwards into the thundering black clouds and disappeared in a flash of lightning.

'Pull that rope.' Hans pointed to a knot of string by Pip's rear paw. 'And release the sail!'

'Why should I?' she said, resenting the rat for being right and ruining her plan. 'I didn't ask you to help me get to France.'

'My apologies, your majesty — were you looking

forward to drowning at sea?' he said, smiling sarcastically with the gale swirling about his whiskers. 'Because I can throw you over the side if that is what you wish?'

Pip scowled and coldly stared into his eyes. Returning her withering look, Hans calmly held her gaze as another clap of thunder sounded above. Neither of them flinched, but Pip crossed her arms tighter to control her trembling limbs. A strong gust of wind blew fiercely from below as Pip's paws slipped on the umbrella handle. Gasping in alarm and grappling the empty air for something to hold, she lost her balance. As she tumbled backwards, Hans immediately leaped forward and snatched her back to safety by the scruff of the neck.

'Wrap your tail around the handle and don't let go!' he yelled. She did so at once. 'And pull that rope or I won't bother saving your life again!'

Putting her pride to one side, Pip obediently tugged at the rope and instantly the polka dot handkerchief billowed in the gale. Grabbing the string in his paw, Hans tied it to the silver handle. As he effortlessly harnessed the wind in the taut sail, the umbrella surged forward and stormed across the water.

'Next stop, France!' he said, his ripped ears blowing in the storm. His leathery scars creased around his face in a smile and Pip realized for the first time that he was handsome.

'Pip,' Hans said, his arms shaking with the force of the wind in the handkerchief. 'Take this and point the arrow to SE.'

He handed her a brass button much like the ones Mrs Smith helped Mr Smith use to fasten his shirt cuffs before they went to church on Sunday. The lid opened with a click. Inside looked the same as a clock face, except instead of numbers the letters N, NE, E, SE, S, SW, W and NW ran clockwise from where the number twelve normally lived. An arrow flickered between them.

Turning until the arrow quivered on SE, Pip pointed her paw out to sea.

'That way!' she cried.

'Listen to me,' Hans shouted over the wind and rain howling about them. 'Whatever happens in the next few hours, if we lose our course we'll end up in enemy territory and I don't plan on dying today.' He stared at the compass. 'You are my guide. Keep SE and we'll reach the Resistance in Normandy. If you drop it – you kill us. Do you understand?'

She nodded, gripping the compass tightly in her paws.

*

All night, Pip kept the arrow flickering on SE and shouted directions whenever Hans went off course, the storm circling above them. The umbrella climbed one towering wave after another, plummeting down the backs of them into dark troughs of water.

As they climbed the crest of a monstrous wave, a furious snarl tore through the sky. In a terrifying explosion of hot water, a scorching, violet dagger of lightning pierced the peak they had just left. Startled with fright, the compass slipped through Pip's fingers and disappeared into the flooded umbrella canopy below.

'What are you doing?' Hans cried over the gale, watching in alarm as the little mouse scrambled down the umbrella handle and dived into the canopy after the compass. 'Tie yourself to something!'

But Pip didn't hear. Taking a deep breath, she plunged underwater.

It was strangely peaceful under the surface, as though she had left the storm behind a closed door. Swimming inside the rain and seawater collected in the canopy, a flash of lightning shone across the surface of the compass where it was lodged between the uppermost ribs of the umbrella. Her chest screaming for air, Pip embraced the compass with both arms and tugged, but it remained stubbornly unmoving. Struggling to pull it free, the urgent need to breathe drummed inside her ears.

As the umbrella climbed another wave, the water inside the canopy rushed backwards and poured it over the side and into the sea. Suddenly the compass popped free, sending Pip backwards through the water towards the canopy's edge. She grappled for something to hold and, making a desperate leap, snapped both paws around the edge of an umbrella rib. Trembling all over, she dragged her sodden body upwards and clambered up the pole to Hans.

'What the hell are you doing?' he bellowed, grabbing her by the scruff of the neck and roughly pulling her to his side of the umbrella handle. 'I told you not to let go!'

Pip was panting too urgently with fear to reply. Above them the clouds swirled together, collecting all their fury in a shuddering fist. As the umbrella began another sickening plunge into a valley of water, the storm threw its deadly punch. A gargantuan bolt of lightning pummelled the wave and the umbrella vaulted into the sky.

CHAPTER ELEVEN

FLIGHT

Somersaulting into the clouds, Pip and Hans grasped the umbrella handle with all the strength they had. All around them, thunder pounded the sky like an enormous drum and Pip winced as the rain whipped her fur.

'Hold on!' Hans yelled, seeing her tremble uncontrollably. 'Don't let go!'

But it was too late. As the gale roared, Pip's fear grew. Watching lightning rip the darkness open with hot, jagged claws, her grip on the umbrella handle failed.

'No!' Hans cried, leaping after her.

Dangling with his tail still wrapped around the umbrella handle and catching her just in time, he carried her by one paw above the furious water below. Another crash of thunder threw them downwards. Grazing the crest of a wave, salty seawater stung their eyes before a sudden gust of wind burst inside the canopy and into Hans's sail.

'Climb up!' Hans cried, eyes gleaming with adventure. 'Now!'

Pip struggled breathlessly upwards and clambered over him, quickly wrapping her tail and both arms tightly around the righted umbrella handle. The rat followed her, effortlessly pulling himself upright to stand beside her. Snatching the string for the sail once more, he harnessed the strong wind and confidently guided the umbrella into the sky.

'Quick,' he yelled over the storm furiously crashing about them. 'Where is south-east? We must stay on course.'

'I . . . I . . .' Pip stuttered. She glanced down at the waves thrashing below and her whiskers drooped. 'I'm sorry. I couldn't hold on to it.'

'What?! We could be flying straight into the enemy for all we know!'

'I'm sorry, I couldn't help it!' she shouted over the gale. Her chest grew tight with shame and she winced at the sight of his jaws hardening in frustration. 'I didn't mean to!'

'I have an idea,' he said after a pause. 'But if you don't do as I say, I'll throw you over the side.' Pip nodded earnestly – he had saved her life three times since they met and she wasn't about to argue with him now. 'Take this –' he handed her the end of the rope that tied the lower part of the sail to the umbrella handle – 'and when I say pull,' he said, taking the corresponding rope for the upper sail in his own paws, 'you do it with every muscle in your body!'

As he loosened the handkerchief, the umbrella instantly buckled as it lost momentum and dropped through the air. The sail violently rippled and flapped, battling against the howling gale.

'Ready?' Hans cried and his eyes glowered with determination.

Pip nodded and took a deep breath as a fresh gust of wind swirled around her whiskers.

'PULL!'

They yanked the ropes with all their strength, and the umbrella rocketed upwards into the black clouds. Blindly hurtling through the thick blanket of damp and gloom, Pip yelped, feeling the rope burn into her skin.

'I can't hold on much longer!' she cried, scrunching her eyes closed in agony. 'I'm not strong enough!'

'Don't let go!' Hans yelled through gritted teeth, his arms shaking as they struggled against the sail shuddering dangerously against the force of the wind. 'Not yet!'

Just as Pip feared her strength would fail her, suddenly clear air filled her lungs. The wind was no longer in a fury and the bite of the rope in her paws ceased. Daring to open her eyes, her mouth fell open in astonishment. All around her were endless white stars blinking in the night sky.

'Now you can let go,' Hans said, smiling with relief.

Gently prying away Pip's fingers, he took the rope from her. Tying it to the umbrella handle, the sail grew taut and the umbrella flew steadily over the rumbling storm clouds below.

'You see those three stars strung together in a line?' he said, pointing into the clear night sky. 'That's Orion's Belt. Now look directly under the middle star. That star is Orion's Sword. It will guide us south to Normandy.'

Fascinated, Pip gazed into the night. In London, she knew the stars were there but they never shone like this and she had never seen them this way before. Shapes were everywhere.

'Now, look behind you,' Hans said, turning with her. 'There's a saucepan over there made up of seven stars, can you see it?'

She scanned the moonlit sky and sure enough, seven stars made an outline of a saucepan, jauntily tipped downwards as though it was filling up with water.

'That is Ursa Major. Now find the top point of the bowl,' he continued, pointing to it. 'And look up to the right. Do you see the little upside-down saucepan?'

She nodded, entranced.

'That is Ursa Minor. At the end of the handle, where it's brightest, is the North Star. Now you can find north and south, you will never lose your way.'

Hans looked into Pip's delighted face and they smiled at one another, both enjoying the endless display of stars gleaming all around them and the calm silence they brought after the storm. After holding her gaze a moment longer, the rat turned away with a tug of the handkerchief, sailing the umbrella swiftly southwards through the night sky.

'Why are you helping me?' Pip said, plucking up the courage to ask him. 'Is it just because you want to go back to Germany?'

'I am an orphan too, Pip,' the rat said after a solemn pause. 'I didn't have anyone to help me when my family died and it was my grief and loneliness that made me vulnerable to the enemy. I got away just in time.' Hans's expression softened. 'I don't want that to happen to you. I'll take you to your family in Italy and then I will return to Germany to finish the fight once and for all.'

Pip didn't dare ask more, feeling his reluctance to speak cool the air around her. She had hoped he would tell her his story, but glancing at the silvery scars torn across his fur, part of her feared knowing exactly what had happened to him. Etched into his skin forever, the violent, jagged lines cried out with suffering and filled her heart with sadness.

As the night drew on, the storm faded into the distance behind them and soon all was quiet as though they were the last two living creatures in the world. With only the sound of the wind whistling in her ears, Pip's eyes grew heavy, her head bobbing up and down with fatigue, until she spotted a tiny white light blink from below.

'What's that?' she said, suddenly feeling wide awake. She pointed her paw down to a white dot blinking in the dark ahead of them. 'Down there. Look!'

'Ha! It's a lighthouse!' Hans said with a broad smile. 'We made good time. This storm was lucky after all.'

Pip scowled in disagreement.

'It's Normandy!'

'How do you know?'

'Because the lighthouse is on – it's guiding the Allied boats to the French coast, just like Bernard said.'

'We made it!' Pip said, leaping up on the umbrella handle with excitement.

'Not yet, Pip,' Hans said, gravely shaking his head. 'The danger is only just beginning.'

CHAPTER TWELVE

NORMANDY

Pip's nose twitched inquisitively as they flew closer to shore, flying over countless black battleships gently bobbing on slumbering seas. Ahead lay a wide stretch of sand with stark metal crosses peppered along it, the first indigo belt of sunrise revealing the jagged outline of black treetops silhouetted along the horizon beyond. The lighthouse stood taller than anything Pip had seen before and seemed to graze the brightening sky with its dependable, blinking light, protectively watching the night give way to the lofty morning clouds.

'We need to land over there,' Hans whispered, pointing his paw behind the lighthouse where a small farmhouse stood at the edge of a forest. 'Noah's Ark is somewhere inside those woods. We must reach it before the humans see us.'

The wind dwindled as they descended through the air and no matter how hard Hans harnessed it into the sail, the breeze collected heavily inside the canopy. Before, the umbrella had confidently stormed through the sky, but now it moved with little more than a glide as it drifted over hundreds of khaki tents, tanks and trucks parked on the beach. Dotting the war-torn landscape beyond them stood rows of upright rifles. The gun barrels were buried in the sand with metal army helmets sombrely resting on top of the rifle butts. Seeing the size and shape of the mounds of earth beneath them, Pip's whiskers drooped with sorrow thinking of Mr and Mrs Smith's son, Peter. She hoped with all her heart that none of these makeshift headstones belonged to him.

Pip gasped as a cockerel crowed. The farmhouse chimney had crept directly into their path as they approached the roof. Hans yanked the sail, but the silver handle scraped harshly against the brick stack, knocking the umbrella backwards into the grey slate roof with a crash.

Pip squeaked loudly in alarm.

'Shhh!' Hans scolded, covering her mouth with his paw as the umbrella ground to a stop, precariously hanging by its canopy from the peak of the roof. A dog growled and barked from inside the farmhouse and in a nearby field, cows looked up from where they grazed in surprise. Pip and Hans froze, hearing thudding footsteps before a door swung open, banging against a wall as a black and white sheepdog rocketed from inside the house.

'*Quoi? Quoi?*' the farmer cried over the dog's incessant barking. His grey hair was scattered madly upon his head with sleep and he impatiently wrapped his dressing gown about him to ward off the early morning chill. 'What is it?'

Pip and Hans held their breath, both terrified their clamouring hearts would give them away. The sound of the breeze rustling through the nearby trees echoed the waves lapping the shore, and the farmer, seeing and hearing nothing out of the ordinary, dragged the dog inside by its collar and slammed the door closed behind him.

'We need to run and jump off this roof,' Hans said, immediately leaping to his paws and pointing to the first wisps of white clouds in a tangerine sky. 'The sun is rising and we are sitting ducks if we stay here. We need cover from the forest, and GI Joe is waiting for us there with the Resistance.'

'All right.' Pip nodded, staring into the thick, rugged woodland, wondering how many creatures lurked there unseen. 'But if we're to get a good glide we'll need a good run-up from the highest part of the roof. Come on!' she said, hurrying up inside the open umbrella canopy with Hans at her heels. 'Now push!' she cried and the rat joined her, shoving the umbrella along the peak of the roof with their paws. As it scraped roughly along the slate tiles, Pip's chest grew tight with fear, hearing the sheepdog bark angrily from inside the house once more.

'Get ready to jump,' Hans said. 'One . . . Two . . . Three. Go!'

As the umbrella tipped over the edge of the roof, they leaped to the metal stretchers inside the canopy and dangled from them, swinging back and forth. The open umbrella instantly filled with air, silently gliding into the trees and finally coming to rest on a bed of brown leaves.

'Follow me,' Hans said, swiftly climbing out of the umbrella. 'Let's close this thing and get out of here.'

Hurrying, Pip pressed the secret carved fig leaf

again, and collapsed the canopy. Carrying it above their heads, they scurried across the ground into the wilds ahead. A throng of trees loomed above them, creaking one after another as if quietly talking to each other in a secret language. Ground ferns trembled with disturbance, scattering early morning dew drops to the earth. Something was moving swiftly alongside them on the ground.

'What was that?' Pip said, hearing a rustle beside her.

'Nothing,' Hans said, quickening his pace. 'Keep moving.'

Suddenly a low growl sounded and a flash of grey fur exploded from the undergrowth, throwing Hans out from beneath the umbrella. As it flew from Pip's grasp, she cowered in horror, watching a tabby cat leer over Hans as he lay stunned on the ground.

'What a juicy rat,' the cat purred, rolling her 'r's and licking her lips. '*Délicieux.*'

'Stop!' an eagle cried, flapping his powerful speckled wings and landing on the ground next to the cat with a limp.

A slim white pigeon settled next to him and fluttered her eyelids. Looking Hans up and down, they all recoiled at his scarred face and body. With a gasp, Pip stepped backwards and hit a wall of fur. Blocking her path was a tall, muscular rabbit, looking down his twitching nose at her. Another hopped beside it from the undergrowth while squirrels stared from lofty branches, flicking their bushy red tails.

'Don't touch them until Madame has spoken to them,' the eagle said firmly. 'They may have information.'

'Wait! 'Let me explain,' Hans said with beads of sweat bubbling on his brow. Hearing his accent, the cat growled and tightened her claws around his chest.

'A German!' she hissed, and curled her lips around her white fangs.

'Enemy spies!' the eagle cawed, and his golden eyes narrowed with fury.

'No!' Pip cried. 'We've come from London.'

'Silence, traitor!' the cat snarled, and her eyes dilated with savageness.

'Take them to Madame,' screeched the eagle. 'Now!'

CHAPTER THIRTEEN

THE HOLLOW

The eagle and the pigeon snapped the umbrella in their talons and burst upwards above the treetops. Leaping on Pip and Hans, the other animals tied their paws tightly behind their backs with twine. The rabbits took positions either side of them, the cat following from behind, her tail swishing from side to side. Hans gave Pip a look that silently told her not to be afraid, but his eyes were wide with unease and she felt the sting of tears in her own. The rabbits pulled black hoods over their heads and the world before them disappeared. Shoved forward, Pip walked blindly on, hearing muffled yells of protest from Hans beside her.

For what seemed like hours, Pip felt the crunch of dead leaves under her paws until the air grew thick with a woody smell. She was pushed through a wall of twigs that scratched against her fur and her ears pricked, hearing the familiar sound of Morse code.

'What is this?' a female voice said, bristling with alarm, and the *dits* and *dahs* stopped at once. 'Who are they?'

'Germans,' one of the rabbits said, ripping off Pip and Hans's hoods. 'The sheepdog sounded the alarm and we found them at the edge of the forest.'

Pip blinked. They were inside a large hollow underneath a fallen oak tree. Its thick, leafy boughs created an oval chamber and the morning light dappled the crisp ground with a rippling white honeycomb. A bullfinch crouched in a large nest concealed in the upper branches, wearing the same headphones and holding the same triggers Pip had seen in Bernard Booth's hideout in London. Directly beneath them stood a hedgehog with little brown eyes that creased at the sides with wisdom. She was surrounded by a small crowd of wild rabbits, squirrels, rats, field mice, three beavers and a stag, dipping his grand head of antlers to the ground to peer inside the hollow. The cat sat on her haunches beside them and purred.

'We saw them come down from the sky,' the other rabbit said. 'In *that*!'

He pointed his paw to the umbrella clutched in the eagle and white pigeon's talons, as they dropped into the hideout from above. The birds placed the umbrella on the on the ground and stood to attention. Gazing at it with shock and confusion, the hedgehog scowled.

'Who are you?' she said with all her prickles standing on end. 'Who are you working for?'

'Madame,' Hans said, drawing a deep breath, his voice tinged with annoyance. 'We are on the same side.'

'I'll be the judge of that,' the hedgehog snapped. '*Who* are you working for?'

'Bernard Booth.'

'Bernard Booth!' she scoffed. 'He would never send me a rat and a mouse kitten with an umbrella without warning.'

'GI Joe, the messenger pigeon,' Hans said, furrowing his brow. 'He was meant to tell you we were coming. He was travelling ahead of us.'

'GI Joe?' the white pigeon cooed in a soft American accent and her head cocked inquisitively from side to side. 'Did you say GI Joe?'

'There's been no sign of him,' the eagle said, and

frowned suspiciously, glancing at the white pigeon beside him. 'Nazi falcons are trained to kill messenger pigeons – almost none survive these days. Bernard Booth knows that better than anyone. He wouldn't risk sending his fastest pigeon when he could send a message via Morse code.' He turned to the hedgehog and spoke in hushed tones. 'Don't trust them, Madame. Spies are everywhere. The enemy are trying to infiltrate us. This is a sensitive time, many are still in hiding after D-Day and the Allied advance still rests in the balance.'

The forest animals murmured anxiously and Pip racked her brains for a way to help. Everything Hans said, they didn't accept. She knew he was German, but he was a member of Churchill's Secret Animal Army and Dickin, GI Joe and Bernard Booth trusted him completely. He had a strong spirit and a tender heart and she had to do something to help him.

'*John has a long moustache!*' she cried, remembering the message in the scroll she had stolen from GI Joe.

An astonished gasp echoed in the hollow.

'What did you say?' the hedgehog asked, turning to Pip with bristling prickles.

'I said, *John has a long moustache!*' Pip repeated at the

top of her voice, trying to sound as confident as possible, but she still had no idea what the words meant.

'*C'est terrible!*' a rabbit said under his breath, and his hind leg instinctively thumped the earth with worry. 'How do they know the code?'

The other animals in the hollow looked at one another in alarm.

'Enemy spies!' they muttered.

'No!' Pip squeaked, but none of the animals were listening to her.

'They've intercepted the message from GI Joe!'

'They're here to sabotage the plan!'

'There's only one way to deal with enemy spies!' the eagle squawked with furious, gleaming eyes. 'Take them to the interrogation wall!'

The forest animals cheered. Pouncing on Pip and Hans, they roughly dragged them to the depths of the hollow where the trunk of the fallen tree had been gnawed into a jagged semi-circular cavity. Shoved against it, Pip shuddered at the torn tufts of fur and feathers snagged on splinters of wood.

'Wait! You don't understand!' Hans protested, struggling like Pip in his bonds, but it was hopeless. The gang of animals were too many and too strong. 'Listen to me!' he cried, cornered against the wall. 'We are here to help you!'

'Stop!' Pip cried, searching for a way to escape, but the animals surged forward, baring their teeth and claws. 'We are on your side!'

'Nothing you can say can save you now,' the cat hissed, curling her lips around her pointed fangs.

Pip glared into her savage dilated eyes, trying to ignore the fear trembling under her fur.

'Back off, you stinking hairball!' Pip spat, ignoring the cat's tail swishing from side to side. A long, low growl sounded from inside the cat's throat. 'We haven't done anything wrong!'

The eagle leaped towards her, furiously beating his wings. Cowering in alarm, Pip scrunched up her eyes as her ears and whiskers blew about her face.

'Leave her alone!' Hans cried. 'What if I told you that I once was a Nazi? A Goliath Rat!'

The forest animals snapped their attention away from the little mouse at once and roared with anger. Hans's words struck Pip like a blow to the heart.

'I didn't know what I was getting into,' he said, turning to her before facing the snarling mob. 'I hate the enemy and I can tell you why! When you hear what I have to say, you will see we are not a threat to you!'

'Stop!' the hedgehog said, her brown eyes blazing with authority. 'If we don't listen to their defence then we are no better than those we hate.' The gang of animals loosened their grips and begrudgingly backed away from the prisoners. 'Speak then, rat,' she said calmly. 'But I warn you, if you lie, I will have no control over what happens to you.'

'If you don't believe me,' Hans said, breathing heavily with distress, 'then you can gladly kill us both.'

CHAPTER FOURTEEN

HANS DER SIPPE EIBSEE

'Not so long ago,' Hans said, ignoring the other animals and speaking to Pip, her eyes stinging with betrayal, 'I lived under the roots of a tree by Lake Eibsee, a place in Bavaria where the water is so clear it mirrors the sky and the snow-topped mountains behind. That was until one winter brought ice as hard as stone to the lake. Soon, no birds sang in the treetops. No deer roamed through the forest and no creatures foraged on the ground. We starved. I buried every member of my family and I was orphaned and alone, facing the starvation that had killed them all.

'With what strength I had left, I walked east to find help. But the path was harder than I ever imagined. The wind bit through my bones. It gouged at my eyes with a thousand claws and every step was a peak I was not strong enough to climb. I can't tell you how far I walked before I collapsed in the snow and my exhausted journey drew to a hopeless end.

'Two days later, I woke in a sewer beneath the town of Grainau, beside a rat as big as a small dog, with auburn fur like mine, but as strong as three rats from my clan. His ruby-red eyes sent a shiver down my spine. His name was Herr General and he had rescued me from the snow. The general nursed me back to health, all the while telling me of Germany's suffering, convincing me that we needed to help the humans find freedom and glory. Youth, loneliness and grief are the meat evil feeds on, and when I recovered my strength, I followed him to battle for the Fatherland, joining his army of Goliath Rats. I felt I understood honour, justice and brotherhood.

'But I soon learned what it really meant,' Hans continued after a long sigh, gravely looking into the distance as if he had stepped into the past. 'We stowed away inside vans carrying supplies north to a human concentration camp. Herr General sent us to prey on the innocent people inside, biting them and spreading fleas to infect them with disease. I am still haunted by the cruelty I saw them inflict and I quickly realized I had to do something. I ran away, hiding inside pipes and gutters, only reappearing to bite Hitler's guards, doctors and officers instead. I made their lives as difficult as I could, chewing through the brake cables in their cars and motorbikes and through the wires of their radio and telephone lines.

'One night when I was taking potato peelings I had stolen from the camp kitchen to give the inmates inside their barracks, I found Herr General and two more Goliath Rats attacking a woman, too weak to move from where she lay. A deadly fury stirred in my heart and a bitter fight broke out. The Goliath Rats began hunting me, but I escaped, stowing away in a Nazi officer's truck travelling across the German border into France. Soon after, I sneaked on to a British Lysander plane collecting members of the French Resistance to take to London. I have served Churchill's Secret Animal Army ever since.'

A strong sea breeze blustered through the forest trees and as Hans paused, his eyes blazed under his scars with the memories of his past. Surrounding him and Pip in the hollow under the fallen tree, the forest animals stood captivated by his story.

'Enough!' the eagle squawked, furiously flicking his gold eyes from one animal to the next. 'I cannot listen to another word. He is manipulating us! He admits it! He is a Goliath Rat! He'll lead them to us all!'

'Leave him alone!' Pip squeaked, annoyed by the forest animals nervously murmuring to one another. 'He's telling the truth!'

'Little wretch!' the eagle cawed, limping towards her.

'Get away from her!' Hans cried, shielding Pip's little body with his own.

'Axis rat *bâtard*!'

The eagle darted for him with his sharp, hooked beak glinting in the dappled sunlight. He was a whisker's breadth from Hans when a sudden clattering sounded, followed by a torpedo of grey feathers bursting headlong into the eagle, somersaulting him away from the interrogation wall.

'GI Joe!' the white pigeon cooed, rushing to her mate lying dazed on top of the stunned eagle and smothering him with kisses. 'It's so good to see you again.'

'Hey, baby,' he cooed in return, his velvety American voice cracking with pain. 'How you doin', jitterbug?'

'We are very happy to see you again, *mon ami*,' the hedgehog said, hurrying to him and helping him to stand. Dumbfounded, the eagle peeled himself from the earth alone and stared at GI Joe. 'We feared the enemy falcons were too many to outrun after D-Day.'

'You're not wrong, Madame Fourcade. I barely made it past those dodos myself.' He glanced at Hans and Pip pushed against the interrogation wall and smirked. 'I'm glad you made it here in one piece, buddy – I see you've made a good first impression.'

'Do you know this rat?' the hedgehog said urgently.

'Sure I do. I've known this hairball since he first joined Churchill's Secret Animal Army. He's on our side and so's the liddle lady.'

'Release them at once!' Madame Fourcade said, her stern brown eyes flashing impatiently from left to right.

The forest animals scrambled to the prisoners and untied the ropes around their wrists. Furiously snatching away her paws, Pip tenderly rubbed her wrists where the ropes had burned the skin under her fur.

'Courtesy of Mr Bernard Booth, ma'am,' GI Joe said, unhooking the messenger canister from his ankle and passing it to the hedgehog.

'*John has a long moustache*,' the hedgehog read aloud with a smile. 'This little mouse was right. Plan Violet and Operation Popeye can begin. Bring me a grape!' She turned to a squirrel, who dashed away at once to burrow in the ground a few paces away. Included with the original scroll was another blank sheet of paper Pip had not seen. As the hedgehog laid it flat on the ground the squirrel returned, handing her a wrinkled green bulb. Tearing the fruit open, Madame Fourcade rubbed it against the paper, revealing hidden instructions and diagrams.

'Invisible ink,' Hans whispered to Pip.

'It appears this rat and mouse kitten's arrival demanded radio silence,' the hedgehog said after reading the words on the paper. A fierce look of concentration passed over her face before she rolled it tightly closed again. 'Destroy it,' she said firmly, handing it to the squirrel, who feverishly ripped it to shreds with his claws. The hedgehog looked Hans and Pip up and down. 'Bernard Booth believes if a Morse code message was intercepted, the enemy would never cease hunting an umbrella mouse.'

'Hans and I are assigned to the mission with you,' GI Joe cooed. 'You can trust him completely, Madame, his being German and a former Goliath Rat has made him one of our strongest assets.'

'You're telling me that Bernard Booth has one of the most feared Axis animal soldiers in his command?' The hedgehog frowned. Noah's Ark muttered to one another nervously and scowled in Hans's direction. 'And he trusts him?'

'It sounds cuckoo when you say it like that,' GI Joe said. 'But I gotta tell you, I'd sacrifice every feather on my body for him. We've completed ten missions together and we're a force to be reckoned with. If anything goes wrong, he pretends to be the enemy and it's saved my beak more than once.'

'And what about this mouse kitten and the umbrella?' Madame Fourcade said, shaking her head in disbelief. '*Mon dieu*. Whatever will these British agents think of next?'

Pip stood tall, trying to look as grown-up and capable as possible.

'Pip's an honorary member of Churchill's Secret Animal Army,' GI Joe said. 'Bernard Booth's ordered that the liddle lady and her umbrella stay in our care and she's to help us while she's here. She and Hans will continue east after Noah's Ark's completion of Operation Popeye.'

'Bernard Booth is full of surprises today,' the hedgehog said with a sigh. 'So, little one – you know that also means you and Hans are also honorary members of Noah's Ark?'

A rush of excitement pulsed under Pip's fur. Now she was a spy in Churchill's Secret Animal Army, getting to Italy would be easy and fighting alongside Noah's Ark on the way didn't seem so bad. She wanted to help bring an end to the war that had killed Mama and Papa.

'*Alors*. We must organize our plans at once, but first,' Madame Fourcade said softly, looking Pip and Hans in the eye. 'Forgive us for your treatment. You must understand that enemy spies are everywhere and we can never be too careful in these times of invasion. I hope we can be friends.' She held out her paw. 'As GI Joe said, my name is Madame Fourcade, I am the leader of this group – Noah's Ark.'

'I'm Pip,' Pip said, tentatively shaking paws. 'Pip Hanway.'

Hans shook the hedgehog's paw in silence.

'Welcome to the French Resistance, Hans and Pip. We are pleased to have you with us.'

The cat yawned with disinterest and the eagle scoffed in the corner with an angry ruffle of his feathers. Used to his temper, the hedgehog ignored him and, climbing on to a log before rows of ears pricked high upon feathered and furry heads, she addressed the hollow.

'Tonight is the night!' Madame Fourcade said, her

141

voice increasing in volume, encouraging her troop like an army general sending soldiers into battle. 'I told you before France fell that Hitler is not unbeatable nor is he eternal! We must continue to nibble away at the enemy!

'After our Allied success on D-Day, the enemy is retreating inland. But we have not won the war yet. Bernard Booth in Stronghold has intercepted a message from the enemy and we're going to stop them.'

'Stronghold?' Pip whispered to Hans.

'It's Noah's Ark's codename for London, liddle lady.' GI Joe winked. 'Don't worry, you'll soon get the gist.'

'This evening we shall conduct Operation Popeye,' the hedgehog continued. 'The humans are moving weapons and laboratory equipment by train east to the Nacht und Nebel camp in the Venteux Mountains. If we let them pass, they will travel to Germany and from there, they will gain strength. They will use the weapons on our Allied soldiers in France, Belgium and Italy. They will take the laboratory equipment to their concentration camps here in France, Germany and Poland. Innocent men, women and children will suffer. But we will not let them pass!'

The forest animals nodded with determination and a proud smile drew across the hedgehog's face.

'When the moon is at its highest, the train will cross Nouveau Bois Bridge over the river beside the monastery at Bec. We will chew through the supporting beams and force the train into the water! Whatever happens, the flame of the French Resistance must not and will not die!'

Noah's Ark cheered. Madame Fourcade paused, feeling stronger with every word.

'Émile,' she said, pointing to the largest of three beavers sitting in the middle of the group. 'Go to Nouveau Bois Bridge with your wife and son now! Gnaw every timber column on the far side of the river into a point, but be careful not to chew all the way through. I will meet you there tonight when the monastery bell strikes twelve and together we will watch the train fall.'

Émile nodded and promptly scurried out of the hollow with the other two beavers at his heels. Pip watched their large, waxy oval tails vanish through the forest's trembling ground ferns, feeling a tremor of excitement beat inside her chest.

'But first,' the hedgehog said, turning her prickled head to Pip and Hans with twinkling eyes, 'it's time our new members proved their worth.'

CHAPTER FIFTEEN

NOAH'S ARK

Nerves fluttered Pip's whiskers as every animal in Noah's Ark turned and tittered with enthusiasm, staring at her and Hans, their noses trembling with curiosity.

'How do you think they'll do?' a squirrel whispered.

'He looks tough,' another said, looking at Hans's lean, scarred body. 'I'm not so sure about her – she looks a little scrawny.'

Pip frowned and stood as tall as she could.

'Don't listen to them,' Hans said. 'Only fools judge by appearances.'

'He's right,' cawed Léon, the eagle, and Henri, the stag, nodded. Regretting what they had said, the squirrels' ears flattened against their heads and they scuttled away. Limping forward, the eagle offered the end of his speckled wing to Pip and Hans.

'Please forgive my behaviour before,' Léon said, glancing at Madame Fourcade with respect. 'I was captured and the enemy left me with scars so I would never forget it.' He gestured to his leg, gnawed and deformed with an unnatural, jagged lump at the knee. 'Every day I feel the pain they caused,' he said, ruffling his feathers with the memory. 'It makes trust very difficult for me, I'm sorry.'

'We share the same scars, friend,' Hans said, taking Léon's wing in both paws and earnestly shaking it. Pip did the same, recoiling shyly from the eagle's fierce, golden stare. 'And not all Germans are Nazis – some of us are resisters too,' the rat continued solemnly. 'Their Fatherland is not my Fatherland. Germany is trapped inside Hitler's snare and I will fight for its freedom until my dying breath.' He looked down into Pip's face, who was staring up at him with a furrowed brow, and a tender smile flickered across his scarred face. 'If necessary.'

'Isn't she a little young to be in Churchill's Secret Animal Army?' the white pigeon cooed to GI Joe, looking up from where she nestled on his shoulder and staring at Pip with an inquisitive flutter of her pretty blue eyes. 'War isn't a place for kittens.'

'I'm old enough to have made it here, aren't I?' Pip scowled, feeling patronized by the bird. She wasn't that much older than her.

Several animals giggled, amused by the little mouse's spirit.

'You've got heart, liddle lady,' GI Joe chuckled. 'The pair of you will get along just fine.'

'I'm Lucia,' the white pigeon said with a smile.

'Pip.'

'Like you,' GI Joe said to Hans, 'Luey escaped Axis capture.' The pigeon gave the rat a friendly nudge. 'But they let her keep her good looks.'

'I was lucky,' Lucia cooed. 'I thought I was done for when they caught me, but then they sent me back with a message to my troops: *Herewith we return a pigeon to you. We have enough to eat.*'

'Never underestimate luck, guts and guile,' the hedgehog said firmly, approaching the group and placing a paw around Pip's shoulder as if she was her own kitten. 'When the worst happens you must use every last drop of them to survive.'

'Then Madame Fourcade has the most luck, courage and brains of us all,' GI Joe said. 'She's escaped captivity not once, but twice.'

Pip looked up at the hedgehog with a curious twitch of her nose. Somehow, she knew every line scored on Madame Fourcade's face told a story and she had no doubt she could be as fierce as she could be mild.

'There is no need to look so worried, *ma petite chérie*,' she laughed, giving Pip a gentle squeeze.

Feeling the hedgehog's warm embrace, Pip's heart grew heavy. It was not long since she had snuggled into Mama's fur, but it seemed a lifetime ago. She couldn't believe she would never see her again and she swallowed, trying to stop tears filling her eyes.

'You are part of our family now. We take the greatest care of one another and strive never to be captured. But it is important for you to know,' Madame Fourcade continued gravely, 'if you *are* captured, your only hope is to escape, either in death or by whatever means you can. Each of us is connected to another animal in the Resistance – that's what makes us strong. We work together, sharing information to destroy the Nazis. But the enemy knows this. They will do anything to make you turn on your allies, and pain can persuade even the best secret keeper to shout and scream.'

Noah's Ark listened in silence, ears flattening with fear against their heads.

'Torture is the most brutal language of war, Pip,' the hedgehog continued. 'You must never underestimate it. Whether you survive the horror of the interrogation or not, the cruelty of it will haunt you for the rest of your life, especially if your friends die by the secrets you told to ease your own suffering. So we must do everything we can to rid the world of evil. Then we can end this war for good.'

'I want to help,' Pip said earnestly, glancing at the umbrella. The sooner the war was over, the sooner the fighting would stop and no more families would be killed. 'I know I can.'

'And you and your umbrella shall, *ma petite chérie*.' The hedgehog smiled and the rest of Noah's Ark smiled with her. 'Bernard Booth has had an excellent idea for it. I want you and Hans to come with me, Léon, GI Joe and Lucia now.' She turned to the others and looked at each of them with a keen determination twinkling in her brown eyes. 'For us to truly succeed tonight, we must conduct Plan Violet.'

'Plan Violet?' Pip said.

'*Oui, chérie*. We are going to sabotage the telephone lines so the enemy have to use their radios when they find out the train has fallen later tonight. Then the

Allies can listen in and learn what else they have planned. Lucia,' Madame Fourcade said, turning to Léon and clambering upon his strong, speckled back, 'take Pip and her umbrella with you. Hans, you go with GI Joe.'

'Climb up,' the white pigeon said, offering her silky wing to Pip. A shiver of excitement rushed under her fur as she sat on Lucia's shoulders. 'This is going to be fun.'

'Hang on tight, liddle lady,' GI Joe said as Hans agilely leaped on his back. 'Luey flies like a devil.'

'But that's still not as fast an eagle,' Léon said, giving Pip a wink.

'We'll see about that!' Lucia said, snapping the pointed end of the umbrella in her talons as GI Joe hopped on its handle.

As the pigeons launched into the air, Pip too began to fly.

CHAPTER SIXTEEN

PLAN VIOLET

Pip had never felt more alive than she did soaring through the air on Lucia's back. Fiercely flapping their wings side by side, Lucia and GI Joe carried the umbrella in their talons and weaved swiftly in and out of towering tree trunks beneath a verdant green canopy of oak leaves. Staring up at the dappled shafts of sunlight dancing through the forest, Pip caught sight of Léon following them closely from above. His white underwings, tipped with long, brown, speckled feathers, stretched wider than the umbrella and beat effortlessly on the gentle summer breeze. On his back, Madame Fourcade leaned her prickled head forward and spoke into his ear. At that moment, the eagle tucked his wings into his sides and charged downwards, elegantly swooping to fly alongside the pigeons.

'Listen carefully,' the hedgehog said, raising her voice above the clatter of wings. 'When you reach the lowest telegraph wires, hook the umbrella handle on one and meet us in the sky above. We'll dive together and pull it to the ground, damaging the telephone line in the process.'

'But will the umbrella be all right? Pip said, her insides trembling with unease.

'We'll see. We've never used an umbrella before,' Madame Fourcade said, her eyes gleaming. 'Get ready, we're almost there.'

Before Pip could reply, the eagle and the hedgehog disappeared, overtaking the pigeons with a burst of Léon's wings.

'Don't worry, liddle lady,' GI Joe said, seeing her brow furrow. 'You have my word. I'll look after this umbrella as if it was my own.'

'Me too,' Hans nodded.

'And me,' Lucia said.

Pip drew a deep breath. With a nervous smile she decided to trust them, but their words didn't stop her heart clamouring behind her ribs.

Ahead, the trees thinned into a wide expanse of grass fields that rolled for miles into the horizon under a clear summer sky. A row of tall timber telegraph poles, connected with long black wires, loomed above rich green hedgerows. Beyond, smoke plumed from distant battlefields. As they left the safe cover of the forest behind them, Pip's ears flattened – she could hear the sounds of gunfire travelling on the wind. A shiver of dread crept over her fur, and she wished the moon shone instead of the midday sun. Sharing the same thought, the birds powerfully beat their wings and tore through the blue.

Nearing the telegraph line, the eagle ascended and hovered above them as Lucia slowed to let GI Joe, carrying the umbrella by its handle, take the lead. Together they manoeuvred its silver hook on to one of the lowest rubber-clad cables, and as the pigeons arced upwards to meet Léon and Madame Fourcade, Pip bit her lip, watching the umbrella gently swing back and forth on the wire below.

'Ready?' the hedgehog asked, staring at them one by one. As the animals nodded in reply, Pip held her breath and tightened her quaking paws around Lucia's feathers. 'GO!'

The birds plummeted through the air and snatched the umbrella in their talons. They furiously flapped their wings, and the timber telegraph poles creaked as the cable stubbornly stretched towards the grassy field below. A moment later it gave way, propelling them all to the ground. Instantly, the pigeons disengaged and soared upwards while the eagle swooped back on himself to unhook the umbrella and carry it into the sky.

'*Magnifique!*' Madame Fourcade cried in delight, flying alongside the pigeons. 'Well done, *ma petite chérie*! Now you and your umbrella are true members of Noah's Ark!' A broad grin drew across Pip's face and her heart swelled, knowing she had done something to help end the war. 'Come – let's do as much damage as we can!'

'Hang on tight!' GI Joe cooed.

Léon released the umbrella from his grasp and the pigeons rocketed downwards, catching it in mid-air. Pip heaved a sigh of relief having it close to her again, and as GI Joe and Lucia hooked the umbrella handle upon another low-hanging wire and ascended again, Pip realized she wasn't trembling like before.

'Ready?' Hans said, smiling from GI Joe's back beside her.

She nodded, feeling dizzy with adventure.

'Now, Léon!' Pip yelled, and the eagle tucked his wings into his sides, charging into the umbrella with the pigeons following close behind.

A sudden growl roared, violently shaking the air over their heads. Cowering in alarm, they looked up to see three fighter planes tearing across the sky.

'Hurry!' the hedgehog cried, gazing fearfully at their metal tails. 'Those are Messerschmitts, if they've seen us we're done for!'

The timber poles moaned as the birds frantically beat their wings. The planes grew smaller and Pip's fur bristled as she watched the middle aircraft break formation. Turning back, its spinning propeller headed straight for them.

'Look out!' Pip screamed.

Fiery shots spluttered from the plane just as the elegraph wire gave way, scattering the terrified birds into the air. Racing back to the forest on Lucia's back, relief pounded in Pip's chest as they entered the shadows, but turning back she gasped in fear. Still carrying the umbrella in his talons and Madame Fourcade on his back, Léon desperately raced for the trees. Behind them, the plane opened fire in a deafening flash of orange sparks. Flying low, the eagle faltered through a spray of bullets and crash-landed in the ferns. The aircraft blasted upwards and thundered overhead.

'Léon! Madame Fourcade!' Pip cried. 'Lucia, Joe, hurry – go back!'

The pigeons and Hans glanced at each other, brows furrowed, and immediately turned around. Approaching the flattened leaves in the thick undergrowth, Pip's throat tightened as she caught a glimpse of the eagle and the hedgehog collapsed on their sides beside the umbrella.

'Madame!' GI Joe cooed urgently, landing next to her with Lucia. Hans leaped off his back and crouched low to tend to the hedgehog, who was curled into a ball.

'Léon?' Pip said, rushing to him. He looked as though he was peacefully asleep. Tentatively putting a trembling paw on the eagle's face, a jolt of fear snapped it back against her body as his huge golden eyes flew open. 'Are you all right?' she said nervously.

'*Oui*, I think so.' The eagle blinked, slowly peeling himself from the ground with a shudder of his wings. Seeing Madame Fourcade's motionless body, he cawed softly and limped over to her. 'Madame,' he said, but there was no reply. The others looked at one another anxiously and bowed their heads.

'Please wake up,' Pip said, feeling the sting of tears in her eyes. Unable to bear the silence, she shook the hedgehog by the prickles. 'Madame Fourcade!' she said fiercely. 'Wake up!'

'Shhh honey,' Lucia cooed softly. 'Let her be.'

'I detest those planes,' Madame Fourcade groaned, uncurling from her ball. Sighing with relief, the others helped her steady herself on her paws. With her heart leaping inside her chest, Pip wrapped her little paws around the hedgehog's soft belly fur. 'Oh, *ma petite chérie*,' the hedgehog said softly. 'Don't worry, I am all right.'

'Jeez Louise, ma'am,' GI Joe cooed. 'You gave us a scare.'

'And myself also,' Madame Fourcade said, standing tall with her prickles trembling slightly. 'Come. Let's return to the hollow,' she said, turning to clamber back on to the eagle's back.

Pip and Hans mounted Lucia and GI Joe and the pigeons took the umbrella in their talons once more.

'Tonight we must be as courageous as butterflies in a hurricane,' the hedgehog said.

CHAPTER SEVENTEEN

OPERATION POPEYE

When the party arrived back at the hollow, the stag, squirrels and rabbits bounded over to them.

'How did it go?' two young rabbits and a squirrel said in unison, hopping up to Pip with twitching noses.

'I think we did all right,' she said, jumping off Lucia's back. Hans gave her a little wink in agreement as he dismounted GI Joe and, smiling, she scampered to the umbrella. Gently running her paws along its carved silver handle and black tarpaulin and finding it unscathed, she sighed contentedly.

'Pip did very well,' Madame Fourcade said, climbing down from Léon's speckled wing and tenderly placing a paw across her shoulders.

'She sure did,' GI Joe cooed, giving Hans a nudge

with his beak. 'And this fella too.'

'We are proud to have you both among us,' the hedgehog continued. 'With two telephone lines now sabotaged, the enemy will struggle to alert one another when the train falls tonight. Let us thank our new friends, and Pip's umbrella.'

As Noah's Ark clapped their paws or feathers together or stamped their hooves, a rosy glow appeared beneath both Pip and Hans's whiskers.

'Hans,' Madame Fourcade said, leading the rat to one side and beckoning Léon and GI Joe to follow her. Pip and Lucia joined them, standing beside Henri the stag at the edge of the hollow. 'Tonight, the train will cross the river through the forest behind the monastery of Bec. It is quiet there – the only humans are monks praying at their beds, so we will go unnoticed.

'GI Joe and Léon, you will drop Hans and myself on the bridge, then retreat to separate trees. The further away from each other the better, we must avoid multiple captures, but keep sight of us while we meet the beavers.' A grave expression crossed the hedgehog's face. 'Remember, Hans, if the worst happens and you are captured by the enemy, every life in Noah's Ark depends on your silence. No matter how badly they torture you,

you must never, ever speak of us or you will be killing us all.'

'You have my word,' the rat said earnestly.

'What can I do?' Pip said, stepping forward. 'Please, I want to come with you.'

'Absolutely not, *ma petite chérie*,' Madame Fourcade said firmly. 'Plan Violet was unexpectedly perilous today and I will not endanger your life like that again. You have already risked too much for one so young.' The hedgehog paused, gently taking Pip's face in her paws. 'You remind me of my hoglets, who I sent to live out the war in a secret place where they could be safe. My heart weeps for them every day but my duty to them, my country and my comrades is inescapable. I must fight for a better world for you to grow up in. War is not a place for kittens. It is time for you to rest now.'

'But I can help,' Pip said, but to her fury, Hans and GI Joe shook their heads.

'It's all right,' Lucia cooed. 'You can stay with me, they'll be back before you know it.'

Pip frowned, feeling her hackles rise.

'Don't worry,' Henri said, noticing the nervous expression on Hans and GI Joe's faces, 'I'll keep an eye on her too.'

'We all must rest,' the hedgehog said firmly, seeing Pip open her mouth to protest. 'Especially before tonight – even you, *chérie*. Now, let's eat!'

The group nodded in agreement and walked together to the far end of the hollow where Noah's Ark's mice, rabbits and squirrels were preparing nuts, berries and seeds in a large pile. As GI Joe and Hans fondly bantered between mouthfuls, Lucia fluttered to Pip, who was eating hungrily beside Henri the stag.

'How did you become a member of Churchill's Secret Animal Army?' she cooed. 'I've never known it to have a mouse kitten in its ranks.'

'That's because you're not a member of Churchill's Secret Animal Army, sweetie.' GI Joe said, gazing fondly at his mate before turning to Pip. 'Liddle lady, Lucia is the most curious creature you'll ever meet. If I had a berry for every question she's asked me, I'd be the fattest pigeon in the world. Remember, *A secret is only a secret if it remains unspoken*.' Giving her a wink, Pip remembered Bernard Booth telling her Churchill's Secret Animal Army's motto, and she vowed to herself she would not speak of them.

'But we're among friends!' Lucia smiled at GI Joe. 'I'm sorry, honey. I didn't meant to pry, I was only trying

161

to make our newest member and her umbrella feel welcome. You've got to admit they're not your everyday spies.'

'The place where I lived in London was bombed,' Pip said, suddenly losing her appetite. She put the nut she was eating on the ground and felt her whiskers droop on her cheeks. 'I lost my whole family that day. The umbrella is all I have left of them. We have lived inside it together like all the other Hanway mice before us for over a hundred years.'

'It's beautiful,' the white pigeon cooed, eyeing its silver handle, wrapped in carved fig leaves and inlaid with gold.

'Yes, it's very rare,' Pip said after a pause, feeling her chest grow heavy with grief. She could still hear Papa's voice telling her their umbrella's history. 'It's one of the first to be used in England and I'm taking it to the only umbrella museum in the world, where we will be safe. My family always dreamed of going there one day.'

'Where's that?'

'It's in Northern Italy.'

Nearby, ears pricked and gradually the rest of Noah's Ark's looked up from their food to listen.

'Northern Italy?' Lucia said, cocking her head in

surprise. 'But that's enemy territory. Why would you want to be there?'

'I'm going there to live with my mother's family.'

'So if you're an Italian, you can't be here as a member of Churchill's Secret Animal Army then?'

'She is as far as you are concerned,' Hans interrupted, staring sternly at the white pigeon. Not a whisker on his face moved and the pigeon blinked self-consciously before looking away. 'Aren't you, Pip?'

He looked over to her and immediately his scarred face softened. The little mouse smiled. She didn't mind Lucia asking about her, and she wasn't sure why Hans did.

'You bet she is,' GI Joe cooed. 'She's the youngest member we've ever recruited. She's damn brave too. She sailed down the River Thames alone.'

'That's impressive,' Lucia said, smiling at Pip. 'And hey, I'm sorry I asked. We've all got our little secrets and don't worry, honey –' she gave her a little wink – 'I won't tell anybody. I'm just so excited to have another girl in Noah's Ark! I hope you and me can be like sisters. Us girls need to stick together.'

Pip enjoyed the thought of having a sibling, especially a daring and pretty one like Lucia. Hans and GI Joe behaved as brothers and the rest of Noah's Ark seemed as close as a family. It made sense for her to have a sister too.

'I'd like that.' Pip nodded and smiled at her new friend, feeling close to her already.

'I am so pleased!' Lucia said, fondly embracing her in her white wings. 'You can share my coop and we'll have fun tonight without the boys. You'll see.'

'But don't you want to go as well?' Pip asked with surprise. She thought Lucia was as adventurous as she was. She was a messenger pigeon, after all.

'Missions are always taken by small groups. It's safer that way. If we were to fail, more of us would die or get captured. Besides, are you sure you'd want to go? You couldn't take your umbrella with you.'

Pip looked at the umbrella and thought of Mama and Papa. It was true; she would never risk the umbrella on tonight's mission. But if she left it in the hollow and sneaked out to watch the mission while the rest of Noah's Ark was sleeping, no one would ever know.

CHAPTER EIGHTEEN

THE TRAIN

Pip woke with a start. Lucia was breathing softly and evenly beside her as she slept with her head tucked under her wing. Blearily lifting her head from her bed of leaves, Pip found all was dark and quiet in the hollow under the fallen tree. But as she drowsily rested her head once more, her ears pricked, hearing the sound of wings clattering nearby. Sitting bolt upright, she stared through the leafy roof of the hollow and into the cool moonlight, shimmering silver through the treetops.

Catching a glimpse of Léon's strong, speckled wings flapping in the dark, Pip hastily leaped to her paws and crept out of the hollow as quickly and quietly as she could. Hesitating for one last look at the umbrella wedged safely beside Lucia, she raced forward and chased the birds carrying Madame Fourcade and Hans on their backs through the forest.

She had not travelled far before a galloping thud charged through the trees behind her. An enormous dark shape vaulted over her, blocking her path on all sides. Standing before her, pointing his great head of antlers down at her, was Henri, flaring his nostrils and stamping the ground.

'No, Pip,' he said, his large mahogany eyes glistening in the moonlight. 'I cannot let you pass.'

'I'm going!' she said firmly, trying to dart out of his way.

'No!' he said, swiftly blocking her path once more. 'It's forbidden.'

Pip dashed forward, effortlessly weaving around him as if he was not there at all. He galloped after her, hopping and twisting across the ground, trying not to crush her under his hooves. As Pip zigzagged through Henri's long legs, the stag stumbled. He fell to the ground with a crash, and Pip skidded to a halt and collided into his flank with a small thump.

'All right! Stop it!' Henri said, panting heavily. 'If I cannot convince you to turn back to the hollow, then I will take you to watch the mission myself. It is not safe for you to go on your own.'

'Fine,' Pip said breathlessly, secretly relieved he would carry her the rest of the way.

'Then climb up and keep quiet. If Madame Fourcade sees or hears us, we will both be in a world of trouble.'

Clutching his velvety fur in her paws, she clambered up his body, scaling the length of his back and up his long neck to the top of his head. Climbing up an antler, Pip smiled with excitement and wrapped her tail tightly around it. Pushing up from his knees and standing tall, Henri cantered through the ground ferns, effortlessly weaving through the trees in great strides that hardly touched the ground.

'We're close,' Henri whispered after a time, as church bells struck twelve o'clock nearby. He slowed, his breath puffing in and out of his nose. 'Those bells are coming from the monastery.'

Pip craned her neck for a better view, but she saw nothing except tall tree trunks creaking gently in the shadows. Looking about, a cold feeling of dread crept over her fur.

'I feel like we're being watched,' Pip squeaked, nervously searching the gloom. As the bells ceased their toll, only the eerie sound of their breath and the breeze gently sighing through the leaves remained.

'These trees have seen more than we will ever know,' Henri murmured, looking into the treetops and quickening his pace, his hackles betraying a shudder of unease.

Hearing water trickle nearby, Henri moved cautiously forward. The forest cleared up ahead in a barren belt through the trees. As Henri and Pip reached it, Léon and GI Joe reappeared above and swiftly beat their wings, quickly swerving to the right. Henri tucked himself behind the cover of the thicket, his ears twitching warily on his head. A wide river glittered in the gloom before them and Pip's heart was in her mouth, watching her friends fly through the shadows towards a timber bridge, eerily silhouetted against the moonlit sky.

'I feel like something terrible is going to happen,' she whispered with a shiver.

'Shhh, it is only our nerves,' Henri hushed, shifting on his hooves.

'But what if it isn't?'

'*Ma petite amie*,' he said softly, looking up at the young mouse wrapped around his antler. 'You must not move or say another word now, no matter how much you want to. If we are seen or heard it could ruin everything for us all.'

Pip nodded, promising herself she would watch in silence, but she could not ignore the fear pulsing under her fur and she bit her lip, hoping the horrible drumming in her ears would soon go away.

The birds reached the bridge and swooped steeply upwards. GI Joe briefly hesitated above it and Hans leaped off his back, hitting the tracks on four paws. Instantly, the pigeon flew sharply to the left and disappeared into the treetops on the far side of the river while Léon swooped low, dropping Madame Fourcade on the tracks in a prickly somersault. The eagle burst upwards to the right and vanished into the forest, not knowing Pip and Henri were watching silently from the nearby thicket.

Hans and Madame Fourcade were racing across the tracks when suddenly Léon squawked from the trees. A moment later, a whistle screeched and Pip felt the quake of the approaching train increase with every breath she made.

'What are they doing?' Pip whispered, fear fluttering in her stomach as she watched Hans and Madame Fourcade frantically dip their heads over the far side of the bridge over and over again. Below, its timber columns had narrowed where they had been gnawed around the water's edge.

'They're searching for the beavers,' Henri said, flicking his tail nervously. 'They should have finished chewing the wooden poles into points by now, so the bridge collapses under the weight of the train.'

'Where are they?' she said.

The whistle shrieked again, making all the animals flinch in alarm. Tearing through the trees beside Pip and Henri's hiding place, the train approached the bridge with its front lamp brightening the darkness like a furious all-seeing eye. Hans stopped abruptly, and looking over to Madame Fourcade, his desperate expression mirrored hers across the bridge. The beavers were nowhere to be seen.

'Émile!' Henri whispered, puffing angrily through his nose. 'Where the hell are you?'

Suddenly a small furry head popped up through the surface of the water beneath the rat and the hedgehog. It was André, Émile's son, speaking animatedly and pointing to the sky with his broad, waxy tail slapping against the river in warning.

'What's he saying?' Pip said, hearing only her heart thumping in her ears.

'Something's happened,' Henri said. 'They have to get out of there!'

The insistent chug of the approaching train drowned out his voice, and the stag quickly shied into the gloom, avoiding its front lamps as they illuminated the trees where they had just stood. A moment later, the bridge shuddered under the weight of the train, carrying eight carriages into the night.

'Run!' Pip cried, watching Hans and Madame Fourcade scramble fearfully across the tracks.

'Run, dammit!' Henri said, stamping his hooves.

Pip could barely watch as Hans and Madame Fourcade frantically sprinted across the bridge. As the train grazed their heels, they hurled themselves from the tracks and crash-landed on the grassy bank.

'They made it!' Pip squeaked, jumping for joy on the stag's antler. But at once she and Henri gasped with alarm. Unknown to Madame Fourcade, Hans and André, four dark shapes with enormous wings and horn-like tufts of feathers on their heads now hovered malevolently in the moonlight above their heads.

'Axis sentry owls!' Henri whispered, shivering with fear.

'Watch out!' Pip yelled at the top of her lungs.

At that moment, the train whistle gave one last

high-pitched scream. Shivering with terror, Pip watched helplessly as the eagle owls plunged to earth with their deadly talons glinting in the gloom. In one brief, savage moment, two owls snatched Hans and Madame Fourcade off the ground.

Instantly André dived underwater with a final smack of his tail, but the other owls were already plummeting from the sky. Fishing him out of the water, they flapped their powerful wings and swooped upwards, joining the two other birds. Carrying their struggling prisoners above the speeding train, they swiftly disappeared into the shadows.

'We have to save them,' Pip said, feeling the sting of tears in her eyes.

'Hold on tight, Pip,' Henri said, galloping back into the trees. 'First we must warn the others. Every one of us is in danger now.'

CHAPTER NINETEEN

FEAR AND FURY

Blissfully unaware of the peril Hans and Madame Fourcade faced, the Noah's Ark animals slept curled up together in the hollow. The rabbits woke first, hearing Henri's fast approach through the trees. Thumping the ground in alarm with their hind legs, the rest of Noah's Ark rose nervously to find the stag and Pip breathlessly push the veil of leaves aside.

'Pip!' Lucia cried in surprise, flying to her on Henri's head and drawing her into her chest with her wings. Pip felt grateful for her comfort and as they embraced, she craned her neck over the pigeon's shoulder to check the umbrella was as she left it, tucked inside Lucia's coop. 'Honey, where have you been?'

'Not now, Lucia,' Henri said gravely. 'There are more

important things to discuss. Is everybody here?'

'Yes, except for those conducting Operation Popeye, of course.'

'The plan has failed,' the stag said. 'Madame Fourcade, Hans and André have been captured.'

All the ears and whiskers in Noah's Ark drooped with dismay.

'Where are GI Joe and Léon?' Lucia cooed, her feathers ruffling with concern.

'They will return soon.'

'What happened?'

'The beavers must have been interrupted by the enemy when they were damaging the bridge. André gave Madame Fourcade and Hans a warning before the enemy seized them all. Have Émile and his wife returned?'

The animals shook their heads and whimpered with alarm.

'If they don't come back then we have to assume they have been captured too. The beavers would never desert us, they've been with Noah's Ark since the beginning.'

'How could this have happened?' Lucia cooed with disbelief.

'There is only one explanation,' Léon cawed, landing in the hollow with GI Joe. Lucia flew to her mate and they fondly nuzzled their heads together. The eagle's golden eyes narrowed with fury. 'Sabotage.'

'Sabotage?' Lucia cooed in surprise. She turned to Léon and scowled. 'What do you mean by "sabotage"?'

'One of you alerted the enemy to the plan.'

The animals in the hollow rumbled in alarm.

'One of *us*?' Lucia snapped. Her neck feathers ruffled defensively. 'Or maybe it was you, Léon. You've wanted to be our leader since day one.'

'Don't be absurd!' the eagle squawked, offended. 'I'll follow Madame Fourcade to the end and I'd gladly die before ever colluding with the enemy. They can take both my legs before I ever tell them anything about the Resistance or Noah's Ark.' Looking the white pigeon suspiciously up and down, he limped over to her with his ebony-tipped beak glinting menacingly in the moonlight, golden eyes bitterly narrowed. 'Where are your scars from when you were captured by the Nazis, Lucia? Such an easy escape makes me wonder . . .'

'That's enough!' GI Joe cooed sternly, protectively stepping in front of his mate. He stood tall, plumping his chest feathers, ready to fight the eagle if he had to. He stared into Léon's furious, gleaming eyes without a trace of fear in his own. 'We must not turn on each other.

Noah's Ark has been through too much for us to crack from within.'

'Who's to say it isn't her!' Lucia said, pointing her wing at Pip. 'She could have led the enemy right to us!'

'Me?' Pip said, squeaking in surprise. 'But I'm on your side. I would never—'

'How well do we know her?' the white pigeon snapped, the mixture of anger and fear showing clearly on her face. 'Think about it! She'd be the perfect Axis spy! No one would ever suspect a mouse kitten! For goodness sake, she is Italian and she arrived with a Goliath Rat!'

'He's not a Goliath Rat!'

'See! Look at her defending him!'

Pip shifted nervously under Noah's Ark's collective gaze.

'Invader scum.'

'Luey,' GI Joe said with a low, impatient coo.

'And to think I wanted to be sisters with the enemy.'

'I'm not the enemy!' Pip cried, scowling defiantly, her whiskers standing on end. She clenched her paws into fists, furiously trying to hide the hurt tearing through her. 'And neither is Hans!'

'There she goes again! Traitors will stick together, won't they, Pip?'

'Lucia! I said enough!' GI Joe growled, flapping his wings in a burst of anger. He turned to his mate and furiously stared into her eyes. 'I have known Hans since the day he arrived in London. They are members of Churchill's Secret Animal Army! Leave her alone!'

'All right,' Lucia cooed softly, but her feathers still ruffled angrily around her neck. She looked at Léon and gave him a wry smile. 'Besides, whatever you may think, Léon, no one could have left the hollow and alerted the enemy without one of us noticing.'

'We can't know that for sure,' GI Joe cooed, turning to Noah's Ark, huddled together in the moonlight. 'Can any of us say that we completely know each other's movements?' The animals looked at one another with their feathers, ears and whiskers twitching uneasily in the gloom. 'Did any of you see anything suspicious?'

There was silence in the hollow.

'Perhaps it was just bad luck?' the cat said frankly, sitting as still as a sphinx. 'What if the enemy saw the beavers start to damage the bridge and captured them there and then?'

'Maybe what happened was a terrible accident,' a rabbit said.

GI Joe exchanged a grim glance with Henri and

Léon. They all shook their heads.

'The plan was top secret,' Léon said gravely. 'Noah's Ark may have known the message was coming but only Madame Fourcade knew the words meant derailing the train. With all the bridges we could have attacked in Normandy, how could the enemy have known Nouveau Bois Bridge was our target tonight without someone revealing the plan?'

'But isn't it possible the sentry owls were patrolling the bridge *because* of the train scheduled for tonight?' the cat said, and after a pause a few members of Noah's Ark nodded in agreement.

'Sabotage or not,' Henri said after a firm puff from his nose, 'what we do know is Madame Fourcade, Hans and André are heading to the Nacht und Nebel camp in the Venteux Mountains. We saw Nazi sentry owls capture them and take them with the train.'

'Oh no,' Lucia cooed with a mournful shake of her head. 'Those poor souls.'

'What's at the Nacht und Nebel camp?' Pip said, fearing the worst. She had never witnessed such a bleak silence.

'It's a camp for human prisoners, a day's journey east from here,' Léon said after a sombre pause. 'But our kind keeps prisoners there too. It's a fortress the strongest men struggle to escape from, and they use the same tricks to ensnare us too.'

'Many animal and human Resistance fighters are taken to that place,' GI Joe said with a sombre coo. 'The conditions are terrible and the guards are feared all over France.' He glanced at Léon's deformed, crippled leg, curled under his body. 'Most don't survive the interrogations.'

'Then we must save them!' Pip said.

'It's too dangerous,' Lucia said with a stubborn shake of her head. 'It's heavily guarded and we cannot risk losing more of Noah's Ark.'

'But we have to try. We can't just leave them there!'

'Hans and Madame Fourcade have escaped capture before. Have faith that they can do it again.'

'But what if they can't? I know I can help! I'm small and fast, the guards will never see me.'

'She's certainly fast,' Henri said, remembering the chase Pip gave him in the forest. 'Believe me.'

'No one has ever broken anyone out of the Nacht und Nebel camp,' Lucia cooed, ruffling her white feathers dismissively. 'It's impossible. It will put too many members of Noah's Ark at risk.'

'Then they'll never expect it!' Pip insisted. 'We can use the surprise to our advantage.'

The animals in the hollow mumbled quietly to one another.

'The liddle lady has a point,' GI Joe cooed. 'And she's right, we've never had such a tiny member of Noah's Ark.'

'It could work,' Léon said with a slow, confident nod of his speckled head. 'I know the camp. I have escaped it before and I know where they will be held.'

'We'll never know unless we try!' Pip squeaked excitedly. 'I know we can do it!'

'Don't be so stupid!' Lucia snapped. 'Why are you listening to her? She knows nothing of war! Or the lives she is risking!' She turned to Pip, her face set in a scornful grimace. 'What are you trying to prove, Pip? We all know that you're just a little London mouse kitten – a lonely orphan with a ridiculous umbrella and no home. Your idiot ideas could kill us and those that we love. Just because you have no one doesn't mean we should too.'

Lucia's words were a dagger to Pip's heart. She clenched her jaw, desperately trying to think of something to say, but the hurt she felt tied her tongue in knots.

'They kill everything at the Nacht und Nebel camp, what makes you think they won't murder all of you too?'

181

the white pigeon continued cruelly, narrowing her eyes. 'Do you even know what they will do to you when they catch you? They'll torture you for information. They'll chop off your ears, your whiskers and your tail.' She turned to Noah's Ark, who collectively cowered at her words. 'She'll give all our secrets to them. They'll be led straight to us and everybody will die because of a mouse kitten!'

'No,' Pip cried, trembling with furious hurt. 'I would never let that happen.'

'Stop it, Lucia!' GI Joe growled, seeing his mate's milky-blue eyes flash with enjoyment.

The white pigeon paused, but a gleeful smile drew across her beak.

'Unless you're one of them and you're trying to report back, trapping more of us with you as you go?' she cooed softly. 'What a successful little spy you will be.'

'Leave her alone!' Henri bellowed with a stamp of his hooves, just as Léon screeched angrily and spread his powerful speckled wings.

'One more word, Lucia,' the eagle said, glaring at the white pigeon, 'and I'll deal with you. I haven't eaten pigeon for many moons.'

'I'm sorry,' she cooed, innocently fluttering her eyes as

she flinched under Léon's gaze. 'I'm only teasing. It's what sisters do, isn't it, Pip?'

'I don't care what you do,' Pip said, turning from where she was standing on Henri's head. She stormed down the stag's neck, clambering over his shoulder and the length of his long leg to reach the ground. 'Rot for all I care, because you'll never be a friend or a sister of mine. I'm going to save Hans, Madame Fourcade and André with your help or not.'

With that, she marched out of the hollow under the fallen tree and into the night alone, only looking over her shoulder briefly for one last glimpse of the umbrella.

'Don't you dare take her there!' baulked Lucia, seeing GI Joe's wings spread. 'Joe? Joe!'

Ignoring his mate, GI Joe took to the air, with Léon following close behind. The white pigeon's face fell with despair.

'No! What are you doing?' she cried, flicking her wings erratically in desperation. 'Please! Stop! You'll all die! It's a day's journey from here! What even makes you think they'll still be alive when you get there? We need to stay together, for all our sakes.'

'You stay here where you'll be safe,' Henri said, calmly turning to the moonlit forest. 'If you won't look after your own, we will. And you'd better take good care of Pip's umbrella. If it's not in perfect condition on our return, prepare yourself to be plucked alive.'

'You didn't think we'd miss out on all the fun, did you, liddle lady?' GI Joe said with a smile, swooping past Pip as she stormed through the forest on her own. His strong wings propelled him forward, and he led the way through the trees with Léon by his side.

'Climb on, Pip,' Henri said, catching her up as she grinned triumphantly up at the birds. He dipped his grand head to the ground beside her. 'There's no time to waste.'

Her heart leaped to have the others with her. She climbed up Henri's nose to his antlers once more, and the four of them began their journey to the Nacht und Nebel camp. As each of them felt the thrill of the unknown thump in their chests, Pip thought once more of the umbrella lying safely in the hollow, and hoped Mama and Papa would have understood that she was doing the right thing.

CHAPTER TWENTY

THE JOURNEY

They had not travelled far through the forest before the crack of machine-gun fire clattered in the distance and Henri slowed, walking around a crater in the earth where a shell had recently exploded. With each step, the forest thinned to scattered fallen trees. Those that remained upright stood bleak and bare in the moonlight, with branches that were torn and shattered at their stems. At their feet, small ditches had been dug in the ground for men to shelter inside, some under the cover of fallen fir branches still green with life.

'This way,' GI Joe whispered, flying low to glide alongside the stag, tentatively weaving between the trees with his ears flinching at every snap of gunfire. 'We need more cover. Follow me.'

But as the forest thickened, the battle grew louder.

'I don't like this place.' Pip shuddered, hearing a low whistle hurtle above them, followed by a fearful explosion in the distance.

'Nor me,' Henri said, quickening to a trot. Léon and GI Joe also sped forward. 'Let's get out of here.'

Gunfire crackled again and a tree trunk beside the stag burst into splinters.

'Run!' Léon squawked, urgently beating his speckled wings. 'Run as fast as you can!'

A storm of bullets pelted the trees. Henri galloped forward, zigzagging through trees and hurdling over fallen trunks in a panicked sprint through the wood, flashing white lights banging like fireworks all around them. Another whistle screamed above and the forest exploded in a bright, thundering roar. Hurled forward by the blast, Henri's legs crumpled under him. As he landed in the undergrowth on his side with a painful skid, Pip flew from his head and somersaulted across the ground.

'Henri!' Pip cried over the ringing in her ears. Shaking with terror, she collected herself and tentatively stood on her paws. 'Henri? Are you all right?'

But no sound came from him.

'Henri,' she sobbed, rushing to the stag, lying motionless against a fallen tree. With gunfire fiercely spluttering overhead, Pip tenderly stroked his soft cheek with her little paw as another whistle sounded and crashed in the distance. 'Can you hear me?'

Pip stared at his eyes and ears, looking for the smallest flicker of life, but the stag didn't stir. As a hollow feeling crept over her, she cast her eyes to his stomach and watched closely, desperately hoping it to see it rise and fall.

'Oh Henri,' Pip whimpered as she buried her face in his. 'Poor Henri.'

A horrible, deathly silence followed before a sudden crackling crunch of dry leaves sounded under her paws.

'I'm all right,' he said, moving his head with a groan. 'At least, I think I am.'

'Henri!' she cried and hugged him harder. 'Thank whiskers you are all right!'

'What was that?' he said, trying to shake the explosion from his head with a rattle of his antlers.

'Henri!' GI Joe cried, landing on the ground beside him with Léon. Together they nudged his head further off the ground with their beaks and wings. 'They have a tank – one of the metal monsters. It will kill us all if we don't move now. You must get up!'

'Come, *mon ami*,' Léon said. 'Hurry!'

'You can do it!' Pip said, helping the birds lift the stag's head with her paws. Clambering back up his neck, she climbed behind his ears to the top of his head and stroked the fur between his eyes. 'That's it, up you get.'

Trembling with shock, the stag wobbled to a stand.

'Now run!' GI Joe said, spreading his wings and soaring into the air with Léon by his side. 'Run as fast as you can!'

A terrible whistling screamed in the air about them as a hot burst of light rocked the earth they had lain on just a minute before. With fear still quaking his limbs, Henri's hooves hit the ground faster than he had ever known. Neither he nor Pip dared to look back, both too afraid the explosion would swallow them whole and as GI Joe and Léon swooped alongside, they raced deeper into the forest until only the stag's galloping hooves sounded through the moonlit trees.

It was some time before they slowed, finding the forest thinning around them. A great field of wheat stretched beyond, rustling in the night breeze under a blanket of stars, blinking curiously from the black sky above.

'We must cross this land and continue east,' Henri said, standing inside the last cover of bracken and puffing heavily in and out of his nose.

The birds glided downwards, landing on opposite antlers above Pip, and the four of them stared nervously into the field ahead.

'We need to reach the Fleur Forest by sunrise,' Léon said. 'And we must travel by night. The humans might see us by day. Food is scarce for them during war, they could kill us if they find us.'

'But won't we be seen without the shelter of the trees?' Pip said, her ears flattening at the great expanse of earth and sky beyond.

'We don't have a choice,' Henri said. 'I smell no trees nearby.'

'France is rich with forests,' Léon said wisely, his golden eyes glowing in the dark. 'We won't be unprotected for long.'

'These tall wheat stems will give you some cover,' GI Joe cooed. 'We'll fly ahead, hopefully another wood won't be far away.'

'I have flown this land before. The further east we go, the more forest we will find.' Léon looked down at Pip's furrowed brow, and at once his stern eyes softened. 'Travel swiftly, we will return soon.'

With that, the eagle and the pigeon soared into the gloom, leaving Pip and the stag to step on to the open ground alone.

'Let's go,' Pip said, swallowing a lump in her throat.

Henri nodded, gave a shudder of his tail, and stepped

out into the wheat field, the crop swishing gently in the breeze. Travelling silently, eyes and ears flickering in the dark, searching for danger, Pip watched the wheat toss back and forth like waves in the balmy night air. As the forest faded into a distant silhouette far behind them, an unnatural, low rumble sounded in the shadows.

'What's that?' Pip said fearfully, turning to the noise. 'It's getting louder.'

'I don't know,' Henri said, looking behind him with alarm. He quickened his pace to a trot. 'We must keep moving.'

'Look!' Pip gasped again. 'Over there!'

Two lights flickered in the distance, rapidly increasing in size as they sped through the forest. Reaching the edge of the trees, the lights raced in plain sight along a road, running directly alongside the field. Crouching low, Henri and Pip watched them approach behind a veil of wheat ears.

'It's a van,' Pip said, sighing with relief. 'I remember the sound from London.' She could clearly see the shape of it travelling past them through the darkness now. It was open at the back and a white flag billowed from a pole attached to its bonnet. There was a dark red cross printed in the flag's centre, just like the one Dickin had

had on his search and rescue uniform. 'It looks the same as the trucks parked on the Normandy beaches.'

'There must be a road running through the forest. It means Man is close. We must hurry away,' Henri said, urgently moving into a canter. 'They were probably fighting the battle in the forest before.'

It was then that a yell rang out into the night, sending cold shivers rippling over their fur.

'It's all right, Harry!' another voice shouted, and a man stood up in full view inside the rear end of the truck. He looked out into the night, directly at the stag. 'We're nearly there, just hang on!'

'That man,' Pip gasped in disbelief. 'It couldn't be.'

'Don't worry, little one,' the stag said, watching the truck's red tail lights race into the distance, far away from where they stood in the middle of the wheat field. Seeing the threat disappear, Henri puffed from his nose and slowed to a steady walk once more. 'They've gone now.'

'I don't believe it,' Pip said, not listening to him. 'He looked and sounded just like Peter.'

'Who's Peter?'

'He's the son of the umbrella shop owner, where I used to live in London,' she said, the words flying out of her mouth. 'I thought I'd never see him again. I have to see if it's really him. Quickly, Henri, follow that van!'

'You must be mad.'

'Please! He won't hurt you.'

'I can't risk it, they could kill us both.'

'But I know him. He won't hurt us,' she said, insistently patting his forehead with her paws. The stag gently shook his head and antlers. 'Please, you have to believe me.'

The clatter of wings sounded in the gloom as the eagle and the pigeon returned, swooping through the night and landing on the stag's antlers once again.

'There is a small village ahead,' Léon said, drawing his strong, speckled wings into his sides. 'Beyond it are more woods and meadows, if we continue through the night we should reach the Fleur Forest at dawn.'

'What's wrong, liddle lady?' GI Joe cooed, seeing Pip's whiskers twitching with agitation.

'Did you see that van that just went past?' she said. The eagle and the pigeon exchanged a confused glance and nodded. 'We need to follow it.'

'That's crazy,' GI Joe scoffed. 'We're trying to keep you and Henri away from the humans, not deliver you straight to them. It isn't safe.'

'That's what I said,' Henri insisted.

'Please, I think I know one of those men.'

'A mouse cannot know a man,' Léon said, shaking his speckled head in disbelief.

'But I do!' Pip said. 'We lived in the umbrella shop together. He's a good man and he's an orphan like me. He probably doesn't even know his parents are dead – they were killed at the same time as my own, three days ago. Please, he's my friend. Please, I have to see if it's him so I can say goodbye.'

'Pip, I don't know,' GI Joe cooed. 'It's a huge risk.'

'Not if you take me on your back,' she said excitedly, her mind brimming with an idea. 'You can fly us there. If they see you, they wouldn't hurt one of their own messenger pigeons. We can go and quickly see if Peter is OK and then we can catch up to Léon and Henri and make our way to the Fleur Forest together.'

'It's not a bad plan,' the eagle said after a pause.

'You've got guts, liddle lady,' the pigeon said, his eyes twinkling. Léon and Henri nodded in agreement. 'No doubt about that.'

'Let's go then!'

'We never know unless we try, right?' he said, fluttering down from Henri's antler to the back of the stag's head. 'All right, climb on.'

With a grin that made her whiskers pop on her cheeks, Pip hurried to GI Joe and clambered up his silky grey wing to his back.

'I'm ready,' she said, taking a firm grip of the pigeon's neck feathers in her paws.

'Hang on tight, liddle lady,' he said, stretching his wings. 'Here we go!'

CHAPTER TWENTY-ONE

PETER

Beating his strong, grey wings swiftly up and down, GI Joe soon left Henri behind, carefully crossing the wheat field below with the eagle protectively circling the night air nearby. From high above the land, Pip watched her friends beneath fade into the distant shadows and quickly become as small as one of the stars, innocently blinking all around her. She looked up and marvelled, unable to fathom how many there could be and how much of the world they could see.

'Do you see it?' she said, staring into the gloom below, searching for Peter's truck along the road.

'Not yet,' GI Joe said, charging towards the North Star glinting in the darkness ahead. 'Do you?'

'No,' she said, feeling a tight knot of worry twist

inside her. 'Hurry! Fly faster, GI! It was driving so quickly, I don't want to lose it.'

'You got it!'

Pip felt the power rush through the pigeon's wings at once. She tightly held on to his neck feathers, feeling the wind yank her whiskers as they burst forward. Gazing downwards, her little eyes desperately scanned the darkness.

'There it is!' she cried, spotting a flash of the red rear lights of the truck on the ground below. It was slowing down. 'Do you see it? Down there!'

'I sure do, liddle lady,' he said. 'Now hang on to your whiskers!'

The pigeon instantly stopped flapping his wings and drew them close to his body. Bowing his head, he dived steeply downwards, dropping through the air like a stone. Gasping in alarm, Pip watched the land zoom closer with every second and tightly scrunched her eyes shut with fright. But just as she was about to let out a scream, GI Joe's wings suddenly shot open. As the air caught beneath them, they steadily glided through the night towards a small windmill and a group of old stone barns.

Three soldiers were jumping from the truck and

rushing another man on a stretcher through the large doors of one of the barns. Holding the door ajar was a woman wearing a khaki shirt and long green trousers tucked into army boots. Her blonde hair glowed in the dark from the hurricane lamp she held up to her shoulder. As she pulled the door closed behind them, her fair, gentle face carried an expression of sorrow.

'Hurry, GI,' Pip said. 'We have to look inside.'

The pigeon burst upward and landed on the roof of the barn, which had collapsed on one side. Clambering down from his back, Pip crawled over furry patches of moss growing over the dilapidated roof and, peering through the gaps in the broken tiles, she searched the faces inside.

Two rows of six beds dressed with white sheets lined the floor below. Inside each one was a man lying on his back. Some had bandages covering their heads, arms and legs, while others were missing whole limbs, the stumps wrapped with gauze. The blonde woman hurried between the rows of beds with a pair of soldiers, who were carrying the stretcher away from the collapsed end of the barn. An older woman tended to the two other new arrivals, who were hobbling in pain.

'I'm going in,' Pip said, scampering to a missing tile

where the wall of the barn met the roof. 'I can't see well enough from here.'

'Nor can I,' GI Joe cooed, fascinated by the soldiers below. 'Let's go.'

Slipping through the open gap, they carefully crept unseen along the uppermost part of the barn to the open hayloft, directly above the flurry of people tending to the man on the stretcher below.

'Keep your hand there!' the blonde woman was telling a soldier. His hands and arms were covered with blood as he pressed down on the injured man's upper leg. 'You must keep holding the pressure there or we'll lose him. What happened?'

'Shrapnel,' the soldier said, lifting his head to look her in the eye.

'It's him!' Pip squeaked excitedly. 'It's Peter! I knew it was him!'

'Shhh,' GI Joe hushed. 'Be quiet, liddle lady – the humans will go crazy if they see us in a hospital.'

Pip stared at Peter's kind face. His piercing blue eyes shone through the grit and grime spattered on his cheeks from the earlier battle in the forest. They were not the same as she remembered. It was as if a cloud of upset had been cast over them, like a storm was brewing in the distance.

'It was a Jerry tank,' Peter said, gravely watching the injured man's eyes roll into the back of his head. 'It nearly finished us before we managed to take it out.'

'What's his name?'

'Captain Stevens.'

'Captain Stevens,' the nurse said loudly. 'Captain Stevens, can you hear me?'

The man was silent.

'What's his proper name?' She spoke quickly. 'His Christian name?'

'It's Harry. Harry Stevens.'

'Harry,' she said firmly, kindly stroking his bloody forehead. 'Harry, can you hear me?'

The injured man groaned softly.

'Harry, I need you to stay awake. Do you understand?'

The man didn't utter a word.

'What's your name?' she said, urgently looking at the soldier.

'Lieutenant Smith.'

'Peter, I need you to keep talking to him.' She looked at the other soldier watching helplessly from the end of the bed. 'You – go over there to the supply cabinet. Get me as much gauze as you can carry and some clamps. Nurse Wallis will help you.'

Hurrying to a large metal locker standing against the wall at the opposite end of the barn, he and the other nurse collected a pile of white bandages.

'It's all right, Harry,' Peter said. 'Soon as we get you fixed up the sooner we'll get that nice glass of brandy we were talking about.'

'We must stop the bleeding,' the blonde woman said, tightening the tourniquet around Captain Stevens's upper thigh. He moaned in pain. 'Peter, I need you to slightly lift your hands for a moment.' Blood continued to ooze in a steady flow from the wound. 'Put them back! Put them back!' she said hurriedly and he did so at once. 'And apply more pressure if you can.'

The other soldier returned and, snatching a handful of fresh gauze from him, the blonde nurse pushed it under Peter's fingers.

'You – get his leg and lift it to your shoulder. It will stop him losing so much blood.'

Without a moment's hesitation the other soldier did as he was told, leaving the collected medical supplies between Captain Stevens's feet.

'Pass me that clamp!' She said, motioning to some silver tongs. The soldier swiftly handed them to her. 'Now lift your hands again, Peter.'

He did so and she feverishly tended to the Captain's wounds.

'Nurse,' Peter said kindly. 'Nurse?'

'Wait. I think I've got it! Just hang on, Harry, we're nearly there.'

Peter slowly lifted his hands and rested one on the blonde woman's shoulder. Flinching with surprise, she followed his gaze and looked into Captain Stevens's pale face, staring lifelessly up at the mouse and the pigeon peering down from the hayloft above.

Pip quietly gasped, feeling the cold silence of death fill the barn.

'I'll clean him up,' the blonde woman said softly, with a mournful bow of her head. 'You can put his leg down now.'

As she walked away, the other soldier gently placed Captain Stevens's leg back on the bed. With a sigh, Peter closed his commanding officer's eyelids with his fingers.

'Poor Peter,' Pip said. 'He looks so sad.'

'A damn shame,' GI Joe cooed, gently shaking his head. 'Rest in peace, Captain.'

Wondering what Captain Stevens had seen, suddenly Peter looked up and locked eyes with Pip, peering from the hayloft above. In the moment he took to blink in disbelief, she had vanished from view, lying perfectly still on her stomach beside the pigeon.

'Did you see something?' the blonde woman said, returning with a bowl of water and dipping a fresh cloth inside it.

'Nothing,' he said, pausing to look again. Seeing nothing, he sighed, shaking the unlikely image from his head. 'I thought I saw something from long ago.'

'You should rest a while. My eyes play tricks on me too without enough sleep.'

'What's your name?' Peter said, solemnly watching her lift the fabric out of the water and squeeze out the excess water back into the bowl.

'Nurse Edwards,' she said, tenderly placing the cloth on Captain Stevens's face, wiping the blood away from his broad, handsome cheek.

'No,' Peter said with a kind smile, 'what is your Christian name?'

'Oh,' she said, smiling to herself in return. 'It's Grace.'

'Thank you, Grace.' Peter said, taking her free hand in both of his. 'You are a fine nurse. I know he would have thanked you too if he could.'

She looked up and her blue eyes reflected the warmth in his.

There was a loud thumping on the doors to the barn. Tearing their gaze away from each other, Peter and Grace looked towards it. The other nurse took a hurricane lamp and pressed her face to a crack in the large timber doors before pulling them ajar. GI Joe drew Pip closer with his wing as a group of eight exhausted soldiers stepped inside.

'We need Captain Stevens,' the first soldier said. 'He was brought here some time ago with more of our men.'

'Hello, Private Hartley,' Peter said, briskly walking the length of the barn.

'Lieutenant Smith, sir,' Hartley said with a salute. Peter returned it and the soldier handed him a folded piece of paper. 'We have a location for an enemy stronghold a few miles east of here. Major Adams has instructed Captain Stevens and our platoon to go there and take it out.'

'I regret to inform you,' Peter said, his brow furrowing, 'that Captain Stevens has passed away from the wounds he suffered in today's battle.'

All the soldiers' faces fell.

'Does that mean you're our captain now, sir?' one of

them asked. 'You're the next man in the chain of command.'

Peter paused and took a deep breath.

'Yes, Jonesy, it does,' he said, sombrely nodding his head. 'We leave at once.'

'Pip,' GI Joe said firmly. 'We gotta go now. If these boys are heading east like we are, we need to be ahead of them. It's too dangerous for Henri if we're seen.'

'But this could be the last time I ever see him,' Pip pleaded. 'Please. Just one more minute.'

'No, liddle lady, it's time you said your goodbyes. He's gotta job to do, and so do we.'

Pip looked down at Peter, wanting to remember every line on his young face, the blue of his eyes and the darkness of his hair. She wondered if he knew that his parents were gone. Perhaps it was a small mercy if he didn't; then he'd be saved from the sadness she felt every day.

'Come on,' GI Joe said, nudging her with his beak. 'No time to lose.'

'OK, OK,' Pip said with a knowing flick of her tail. 'I'm coming.'

They hopped back along the uppermost part of the wall of the barn, retracing their steps back to the gap in the roof tiles. Slipping through it and climbing to the back of GI Joe's neck once more, Pip gazed downwards for a final glimpse of Peter, picking up his rifle as he led his men out of the barn and into the night.

CHAPTER TWENTY-TWO

GUTS AND GUILE

GI Joe hurried east, swaying his head from side to side, scanning the earth below for signs of Henri and Léon. As he quickly gathered pace, Pip gazed over her shoulder and felt the sting of tears. Seeing Peter was like stepping into the past and her mind was flooded with memories of Mama and Papa in the umbrella shop. His eyes, once so clear and full of life, had darkened, and she knew that war would have changed hers forever too.

'Please don't let him get hurt,' she whispered quietly, looking into the stars twinkling above her. 'Please keep him safe.'

Shivering with the memory of Captain Stevens's lifeless eyes staring blankly up at her, a teardrop trickled down the length of her whisker. Drooping from the whisker's end for a brief moment, it fell and vanished into the wind.

'Hold on, liddle lady,' the pigeon said with a sudden clatter of his wings. 'We're being followed.'

'What?' she said, feeling the fur on the back of her neck stand on end. 'Who by?'

'I don't know. Another bird is circling us.'

Pip searched the night about them and felt her heart thump inside her ears. Sure enough, a bigger bird was matching GI Joe's speed through the night alongside them.

'It's coming for us!' she cried in alarm, watching the bigger bird's broad, black wings storm through the air towards them. 'Hurry, GI!'

The pigeon bowed his head and swiftly dived through the sky.

'Faster, GI!' she urged, seeing the bigger bird plunge through the air after them. 'It's gaining on us!'

'It's a falcon!' the pigeon said, beating his wings as fast as he could. 'They're the only birds fast enough to catch us.'

Thick brambles lay below, tangled around the shadowy border of a wood. Hurtling through the sky towards them, it was then that Pip realized GI Joe was not going to slow down.

'Whatever happens next,' GI Joe said, panting from the strain of flying, the thorns zooming closer, 'do not let go of me!'

Pip instinctively closed her eyes as the spikes ripped through their skin. Wincing in pain, they tumbled through the undergrowth in an explosion of feathers and landed on the cold earth beneath the brambles with a thump. Pip and GI Joe froze, watching in silence as the falcon swooped and landed on the thorns above them.

Pip trembled, hardly daring to breathe. Staring wide-eyed at GI Joe, her ears cocked, hearing the quiet whimpering of two petrified rabbit kittens, their long ears flattened against their heads.

'We should never have left the warren,' the smaller one was crying softly as though in a trance. 'We never should have left the warren.'

'I wish we hadn't,' the bigger rabbit muttered in reply, trembling all over. 'I wish we hadn't.'

'Shhh!' Pip hushed them as quietly as she could, but the rabbits could not hear her through the panic rising inside their little bodies. 'Be quiet! It will hear you!'

Curling its black head through the roof of brambles, the falcon screeched in delight, its black eyes widening at the sight of prey below.

'It's coming for us!' the smaller rabbit gasped in horror, watching it tear away the thin, tangled branches above them with its strong yellow talons. 'What do we do?'

Pip looked up and shuddered, seeing how quickly the falcon was digging through the thorns.

'We need to find a way out of here!' she squeaked, scrambling under the thicket with GI Joe. But a wall of thorns surrounded them on all sides. 'GI, you could never fit through!' she said desperately, staring at the small gaps between the thorns and feeling despair tighten her chest. 'Maybe I can squeeze through and distract it for long enough for you to fly out?'

'The brambles are too thick above us as well,' he said, looking up into the tangle of spiky branches rapidly being pulled away by the falcon. 'I can't get the speed I need to push through them and fly away. Besides, the cover in the woodland is no better than we have here.'

'Then we're trapped.'

'We must run!' the bigger rabbit cried, its eyes flitting from side to side in terror. It hopped with its friend to the edge of the thorns. 'It's going to kill us!'

'Stop!' Pip said. 'It wants us to run! If GI can't fly out of here, neither can it! Without these brambles we are out in the open, and then we stand no chance against it. We must wait for it to tire and give up.'

'But it's coming!' the smaller rabbit whimpered as shredded brambles rained from above.

A strange sound rumbled, growing louder as it approached through the nearby trees. Hearing it, the falcon turned its head and cawed, its feathers ruffling furiously all over its body. With a bloodthirsty screech, a flash of brown speckled feathers launched headlong into the falcon, tumbling it to the earth on its back.

'It's Léon!' Pip cried, watching the eagle pin the falcon to the ground with his sharp, golden talons.

'You get him!' GI Joe cooed, aggressively plumping his chest feathers.

The falcon flapped its wings, trying to detach Léon's vicious grip upon its white speckled chest. But the eagle was stronger, and closed his claws tightly together. Cawing with pain, the falcon lurched its hooked beak upwards and snapped at the eagle's throat. Swerving his upper body out of harm's way, Léon's golden eyes narrowed. With a fearful cry, he leaped forward. Gasping in horror, Pip turned away. Stumbling backwards, she immediately yelped in alarm as the brambles in front of her were lifted away.

211

'Henri!' Pip cried, delighted to see the stag's handsome face meet hers, peering under a crown of thorns heaved from the ground by his antlers.

'Get out of there!' he bellowed.

'Run!' the bigger rabbit cried to its friend, watching blood drip from the eagle's beak in terror. 'Hurry! Before it sees us!'

'Wait! It's OK!' Pip said. 'He won't hurt you, he's our friend!'

It was too late. The rabbits bolted from the brambles, racing in a desperate zigzag between the stag's legs. Watching their little white fluffy tails flee into the shadowy woodland beyond, Pip hoped they would get home safely, just as a loud explosion rocked the earth. Cowering in alarm, Pip and her friends watched the rabbits disappear in a terrible blast of dirt, bursting upwards from the ground.

'Those poor rabbits!' she cried, wide-eyed with fear. 'What was that?'

'Landmines – small bombs buried in the ground,' Léon said, his wings hunching around his head in surprise. 'There could be humans nearby.'

Suddenly a large, bright beam of light flashed into the gloom, shining through the trees like a furious eye staring into the night.

'Take cover!' GI Joe squawked.

'Henri!' Pip cried, diving behind the thorns with the eagle and the pigeon. But the stag hesitated, struggling to see a place big enough for him to hide. Behind him, the cold glow of the light crept over his tail. 'Watch out!'

Leaping behind the bramble bush, Henri cowered on his stomach as a nearby tree splintered with a deep bullet hole.

'*Was war das?*' an angry man's voice said from the direction of the house standing in the gloom beyond.

'*Es ist nichts, Herr,*' another man said. '*Ein Reh.*'

With that, the beam of light disappeared.

'German snipers,' GI Joe whispered. 'The mines must be a warning signal. When they explode, they know the enemy is close.'

'The house has to be a lookout,' Léon said. 'The upper floors will give them the advantage. They'll easily see movement on the ground from there.'

'Look!' Henri motioned his antlers behind them to the wheat field they had crossed before. 'Men are coming. Over there – they're moving slowly but they're heading this way.'

The others quickly turned and searched the gloom, their ears pricked up. Sure enough, the shadowy figures of men holding rifles at their waists were walking through the tall wheat stems. Distant peals of laughter travelled on the breeze until a voice hushed and abruptly silenced them.

'Did you hear that?' Pip gasped. 'One of them just said, "Yes, Captain Smith."'

'I heard it too,' GI Joe said, his feathers ruffling anxiously around his neck. Léon and Henri nodded.

'That house,' Pip said urgently. 'It must be the Axis stronghold he and his men were sent to destroy. They are heading straight into a trap!'

'And so are we,' GI Joe cooed. 'We can fly over the minefield but Henri has to cross it.'

'I can walk around it,' the stag said. 'I have the cover of the trees.'

'It's too risky. They'll have hidden mines there. Snipers use them to direct men into their line of fire.'

'Then we have to clear a path for Henri and Peter,' Pip said urgently. 'How do they work? There must be a way we can stop them.'

'They are triggered by weight,' Leon said. 'When they are stepped on, they explode.'

'What if we dropped rocks on them?'

'That could work, *mon amie*!'

'I'm small – I could find the mines and you and GI Joe could drop the stones from above and set them off. The Nazis will never know what's happening. Let's go! We don't have much time.'

'Liddle lady, my claws are too small to pick up large rocks,' GI Joe cooed, regretfully looking down at his pink talons. 'Small ones won't explode the mines.'

'Then Léon and I will do it. You and Henri find the rocks.'

'OK, let's get to work!' the eagle said, limping to her.

'No. Wait for me at the edge of the trees. I'll find the mines on the ground first. Henri, you collect the rocks and leave them in an easy place for us to pick up.' She turned to the eagle, standing tall with GI Joe behind the brambles. She had once been so afraid of him but now when she looked into his golden eyes, she felt stronger knowing he was with her. 'When I get back we'll fly over and drop them on the mines.'

'You're the craziest liddle lady I've ever met!' GI Joe cooed proudly. 'It's a damn shame you weren't born a pigeon – you'd make a fine messenger!'

'It's true,' Leon said, nodding his speckled head. 'You are an extraordinary member of Noah's Ark, *mon amie*.'

'I'm only trying to do what's right.' Pip smiled self-consciously.

'And you are doing a fine job,' Henri said, affectionately nudging her with his nose. 'Here,' he said, kicking a rock with his hoof. 'We will find others. I just wish there was more I could do to help you this time.'

'We'll be all right,' Pip said. 'I'll be back soon.'

Heart pounding against her ribs, she leaped over the ground to the shadowy outline of the house, just visible beyond the trees. Leaving the cover of the woodland behind her, Pip's fur tingled warily in the open air, listening to tall trees creaking in the gloom. The grey stone house seemed abandoned, standing in a small clearing ahead, surrounded on all sides by the wood. A dense layer of ivy covered its walls, creeping up its stonework beyond the lower level before spreading into the shattered glass of the three upper sash windows. Searching through the blades of grass, she saw them: unnatural metal discs bulging out of the earth.

Swiftly scampering across the clearing, stopping each time she came to a mine and darting around it, Pip found four buried along the wooded borders of the grass to the left and right of the house. Hurrying back to GI

Joe, Léon and Henri, she found them watching her from the cover of the trees.

'You were right, GI,' she said, breathlessly coming to a stop at the stag's hooves. 'The only mines I saw are near the trees to each side of the house. There are none in front of or behind it.'

'How many are there?' GI Joe cooed.

'Two on each side, so we'll need four rocks.'

'It's possible there'll be more hidden in the undergrowth, Henri,' Léon said gravely. 'Be sure only to run where the mines have exploded.'

'Don't worry about me,' Henri said, pointing his antlers to a nearby pile of stones they had made while Pip was away. 'Hurry, both of you. The men cannot be far and sunrise will not wait for us to arrive in the Fleur Forest.'

'I can carry two at a time,' Léon said with a nod, dipping his upper body low to the ground. 'Come, Pip, climb on to my back.'

'We'll keep you in sight,' GI Joe cooed, watching her clamber up the eagle's wing to sit behind his neck.

'We'll see you soon,' Pip said with a determined smile, trying to ignore the nerves fluttering in her stomach. 'Let's go.'

Léon bent his knees and jumped, smoothly lifting them into the air with his broad wings. Pip's mouth fell open in awe as he swiftly arced upwards, silently grazing the tips of the treetops. Diving back down to earth and hovering above the pile of rocks, he snapped one in each talon before powerfully climbing into the sky once more.

'Fly to the edge of the clearing on the far side of the house,' Pip said, scanning the earth below. The eagle glided over the house to the right. 'Here they are,' she said, patting him gently on the back of the head with her paw. 'Look, down there.'

'*Oui*, I see them,' the eagle called, arching his head and spying the mines hidden in the grass far below. Shivering his wings, he hovered as if taking aim over unsuspecting prey. '*Un* . . .' he whispered, '*deux* . . . *trois!*'

Tumbling through the air, the rock smashed its target, bursting the ground open in a furious tower of burning earth.

'There's another!' Pip cried to the eagle as he swiftly flew out of harm's way along the wooded border.

Fluttering his wings and dropping the other rock, Léon immediately swooped upwards in an arc over the trees and Pip squeaked with delight, seeing the second mine explode without hurting a soul.

'*Wo sind sie?*' A voice shouted furiously from the house, and the beam of light returned, sweeping back and forth in the gloom.

'*Ich weiss nicht, Herr!*' another man said.

'It's working!' Pip grinned. 'They don't understand what's happening!'

'*C'est formidable!*' Léon said, racing back to Henri, standing deep in the thicket, with GI Joe peering out into the clearing from his antlers. Diving down to the pile of stones, the eagle grasped two more rocks in his talons and soared back into the sky.

'Go to the other side of the grass this time,' Pip said. 'They'll never expect it!'

'*Bien sûr!*' the eagle confirmed, turning and flying over the house to the opposite side of the clearing.

'There!' she said, spying the pair of mines hidden in the grass along the border of the trees. 'Do you see them?'

'*Oui!*'

The eagle hovered as he did before, aiming the stone above the metal disc glinting unnaturally in the moonlit grass. Dropping it, he swiftly flew to the next mine and let go of the other rock. But as he curved upwards to fly out of harm's way, only one explosion blasted from the ground. Instantly the beam of light swerved in its direction.

'Damn,' Léon cursed. 'I missed it.'

'Hurry,' Pip said firmly. 'We need to try again.'

'*Finden Sie!*' The angry voice shouted.

'*Ja, Herr!*'

At that moment, the light climbed from the ground and searched the trees above. The fur on the back of Pip's neck stood on end as she saw herself and Léon glow under the cold, white stare of the beam.

'*Ein Adler!*' the voice cried.

A splutter of gunfire thundered into the night. Swooping as fast as he could, Léon drew his wings close into his body and dived towards the trees below.

'We can't give up now,' Pip said desperately. 'We have just one more mine to blow.'

'We won't, *mon amie*,' the eagle said, weaving in and out of the trees.

Now approaching Henri and GI Joe from behind, the stag flinched in alarm, only hearing Léon a moment before he landed on the pile of stones.

'That was a close one!' the pigeon cooed from Henri's antlers. 'You've gotta be damn careful when you go back out there. They're scanning the sky for you.'

'My friends,' the stag said gravely, 'please take care.'

'As soon as you see the last mine explode,' Pip said urgently as the eagle landed on the rocks and clasped two more in his talons, 'run along the border of the wood and the clearing where the mines have blown. We'll meet you on the other side.'

With that, Pip and the eagle burst into the air, turning back the way they came, weaving through the cover of the tree canopy. Shadowy outlines of men were now outside the house, following the searchlight sweeping over the wood with rifles poised at their shoulders.

'Hurry, Léon,' Pip whispered, shuddering at the sight of the soldiers. 'Do it now while the light is still shining on the opposite side of the wood!'

The eagle sped forward and flew into the open air.

'There it is,' she said, pointing her paw to the final mine hidden in the grass below.

'*Oui*, I see it,' Léon said, immediately hovering.

'Drop the stone!' she cried, fearfully watching the beam of light creep towards them over the clearing, but the eagle hesitated, fluttering his wings harder, precisely aiming at his target.

'Now, Léon!' Pip said, seeing one of the men on the ground point at them. The others turned their rifles at once. 'Drop it now!'

Narrowing his golden eyes with concentration, the eagle opened his talons and released his grip on both of the stones, sending them tumbling to earth one after another. As a burning tower of earth blasted into the air, and the eagle soared upwards out of danger, a terrible storm of gunfire thundered through the night and the eagle's wings stopped beating.

'Léon!' Pip yelped, plunging through the sky. 'Léon!'

The grass below zoomed closer with every second

and she scrunched up her eyes, dreading the pain when they hit the ground.

'I'm all right,' Léon said with surprise, catching their fall with his wings a moment later. 'I'm sorry, *mon amie*. That noise was so loud, it startled me. I thought I was hit.'

Pip shuddered, still too afraid to speak. Flying low through the clearing to the woodland beyond the house, Léon climbed again and perched on a tree branch.

'Look!' he said, nodding his speckled head behind them.

Pip turned and gasped. The gunfire was not from the enemy after all, but Peter and his men shooting their rifles from the cover of tree trunks in front and to both sides of the house, where the landmines had now been cleared.

'Here they come,' Léon said triumphantly, watching Henri gallop safely away from the soldiers along the border of the wood, with GI Joe flying swiftly alongside him.

'Time to get ourselves outta here,' the pigeon said, swooping to the tree branch beside Pip and Léon.

'Come,' the stag bellowed from below, puffing heavily in and out of his nose. 'The Fleur Forest is not much further, I can smell it.'

As the eagle spread his wings and leaped from the tree, Pip turned, hearing the sound of cheering from the clearing behind. As she soared onwards on Léon's back, her last sight was of Peter, smiling broadly and slapping the back of one of his men.

'Goodbye, Peter,' she said quietly. 'Good luck.'

Watching him until he disappeared into the darkness, she looked into the sky ahead, brightening with the first violet hues of sunrise.

CHAPTER TWENTY-THREE

THE FLEUR FOREST

An orchestra of cicadas had already started their morning melodies when Pip glimpsed the bluest water she had ever seen. Gently rippling behind a veil of leaves rustling in a soft breeze, it was as if two skies lay one on top of the other. Rich, green trees lined the water's banks and its surface gleamed with pulses of dancing sunlight. Watching the tiny fish swimming in and out of the plants gently swaying in the shallows, Pip thought of Hans and wondered if the lake in Bavaria where he grew up was as beautiful as this one.

'What is this place?' she asked, clambering down Henri's neck as he stopped to dip his great head of antlers and drink. Léon and GI Joe swooped beside her on the sand and bowed their heads to the water's edge.

'We are at the southernmost point of the Grand Lakes of the Fleur Forest,' the stag said, looking up for a moment between sips. 'You must be thirsty, try some.'

The cold water tasted sweet and refreshing and Pip greedily slurped it until she could have no more. Their thirsts quenched, Henri grazed the grass along the banks of the lake and Léon hunted the dragonflies darting over the surface of the water, while Pip joined GI Joe to scour the undergrowth for nuts, berries and seeds. Growing weary with full bellies, they returned to the thicket of the surrounding forest. Scraping the earth flat with his front hooves, Henri settled on the ground with his legs tucked under him and Pip curled up on top of his head. Above them, GI Joe and Léon swooped to a low-hanging tree branch and rolled their wings with fatigue.

'How much further is it until we get there?' Pip asked with a drowsy stretch that made her ears pop on her head. Feeling restless yet exhausted, she struggled to get comfortable between Henri's ears. Her mind was turning somersaults, wondering fearfully what was happening to Hans, Madame Fourcade and André in the camp.

'It's not far.' The stag yawned softly with a shake of his antlers. 'We will arrive very late tonight. Men hunt in these parts, so it's not safe to leave before dark. We'll continue our journey at sunset.' His big brown eyes looked up at the little mouse wriggling on his head. 'Try not to worry, little one, we'll find our friends as soon as we can.'

'How do you know the way?' she asked, liking the sound of his voice. It was calm and comforting.

'I have travelled these skies before, *mon amie*,' Léon said. 'I rested in this place when I escaped from the Nacht und Nebel camp.'

'And I know of this forest's smell. It's famous among deer for its wild flowers – we enjoy eating them the most. I was born in Belgium in the wooded land that grows along the borders of France and Germany and although it's far away, I can breathe in to find my way home. The Venteux Mountains to the south-east also have their own smell, and even if the wind is high and I struggle to find my way, I can use the sun and the stars as my guide.'

'Like a compass?' Pip said, fondly remembering Hans teaching her how to use the sky as one of her own.

'Exactly.' GI Joe smiled. 'So if in doubt, follow your eyes and your nose, then you'll always find your way home.'

'But what if you don't have a home?' she asked with a

mournful sigh, seeing the destroyed umbrella shop in her mind.

'Then your suffering will teach you courage, *mon amie*,' Léon said wisely. 'But you must surround yourself with those that are good, who strengthen your heart for the better. Then the sadness inside you will not fall into darkness. Evil often feeds on those that have suffered the most.'

'Like what happened to Hans? He had lost everything when Herr General found him.'

'*Oui*. He is lucky that his heart is strong, otherwise the Goliath Rats could have changed it forever.' His face softened, seeing her brow furrow. 'Worry not, little one. Now you are with Noah's Ark you are safe. Most of us have lost our homes too, but wherever we are, when we are together we are home.'

'He's right,' Henri said gravely. 'It was the worst day of my life when I lost mine.'

'I'm sorry,' Pip said, understanding his sorrow and tenderly stroking the top of the stag's head.

'I lived on the French bank of the River Meuse. Our forest was so dense, we thought it would be impossible for the enemy tanks to pass through,' Henri said, shaking his head as his voice grew heavy with anger. 'But those metal monsters stormed through it with their soldiers, tearing down our trees and ripping up our earth along a line they say stretched a hundred miles. Then the planes came, swarming above us in the sky like black flies, dropping bombs until there was nothing left. We never stood a chance. When they crossed the river and invaded France, I joined the Resistance so I could fight them from within.'

'Blitzkrieg,' Léon said, angrily twitching his speckled wings with cold, amber stare.

'Like the Blitz in London?' Pip said. 'The bombs came every night for months.'

'*Oui*. Nazi Germany's "lightning punch". They threw everything they had at us, but unlike Britain, we fell. It was our darkest day. They took our country – our home – from us. But we were not defeated. Madame Fourcade and I were the first members of Noah's Ark. As a leader she has great courage, knowledge and understanding. I will never lose faith in her and we will not give up until our freedom is restored.'

'And we've got a lot to thank you for,' GI Joe cooed, nodding at the stag and the eagle. 'Without the Resistance telling us where the enemy was hiding and sabotaging telecommunication lines, trains, roads and bridges, we could have lost D-Day.'

'What was it like that day?' Pip said with an inquisitive twitch of her nose. She had heard about the Normandy landings in the umbrella shop, but Mama and Papa had never wanted her to know too much of what was happening with the war.

'D-Day.' GI Joe cooed a troubled sigh filled with difficult memories. 'Flying over the English Channel to France that night, strapped to my paratrooper's chest, you couldn't count how many boats and planes there were, carrying thousands and thousands of Allied soldiers. Every one of those vessels carried pigeons like me, because radio silence was imperative. The enemy could listen in to radio messages and know we were coming, but they couldn't hear us flying our messages in the sky. We just had to outrun their falcons back to Britain and that's no easy task, believe me.'

Pip shuddered, remembering the falcon and the bramble bush.

'I was strapped to First Lieutenant John Russell from Fox Company in the 101st Airborne Regiment, the best air assault team of soldiers there is,' the pigeon cooed, proudly plumping his chest feathers. 'His mission was to take out the Nazi gun cannons hitting our boys arriving at the beaches. Mine was to deliver their message back to England if they succeeded.

'It was just after we flew over the Channel Islands when the flashing bullets and the missiles started flying at us, exploding like the biggest fireworks display you've ever seen. And we jumped right into that hornets' nest! It was dumb luck not to have been shot and killed on the way down like so many others were – our parachute looked like Swiss cheese when we landed, it had so many bullet holes in it. It was scary as hell, but distraction will kill you and we had a job to do.

'Once the boys cleared the gun cannons, they scribbled the good news on to a small sheet of paper, slotted it into the canister tied to my leg and released me into the air. Flying back to base over the beaches . . .' The pigeon paused and closed his amber eyes with a grave shake of his head. 'I'll never forget it. The ocean was bleeding from the thousands of men who had been hit or killed. The water lapped at their bodies lying on the beach, some of them face down in the sand without their arms or legs. After I'd delivered the message telling Britain they'd won, I heard our soldiers battled until midnight that night. And they're still fighting to this day, but you can be sure they're gonna storm through

Hitler's front door in Berlin. Just you wait.'

Pip didn't know what to say. Only a few weeks ago, thousands and thousands of men had perished at the same place she and Hans had arrived on the Normandy coast. She thought of Peter and couldn't imagine how terrified he must have been there. Nor could she comprehend how frightened Hans, Madame Fourcade and André must be at that moment, and she shivered, remembering what Lucia had said about torture before they left the hollow under the fallen tree.

'How much longer will the world fight for?' she said, feeling a knot of worry tying tightly in her stomach.

'We all must hope and pray it will end soon,' Henri said.

'Amen to that,' GI Joe cooed.

With those last words, silence fell on Pip and her friends as they gradually drifted into a fitful sleep, feeling the weight of the night to come tremble uneasily in their hearts.

CHAPTER TWENTY-FOUR

THE CAMP

'Wake up, Pip,' GI Joe said, gently nudging her with his beak where she lay asleep, curled up on top of the stag's head. She lifted her head groggily. 'We gotta go.'

Opening her eyes, she found a ghostly mist had crept over the lake, lingering on its surface like delicate clouds. Night had fallen and the frogs were softly croaking along the edge of the water, with black bats swooping and diving above them, feasting on insects in the shadows.

'Let's go,' she said, shaking the sleep from her whiskers with a frown. 'Why didn't you wake me sooner?'

'We were asleep too,' Henri said, lurching forward to a stand with a shudder of his tail. 'We travelled very far yesterday, we all needed the rest.'

'Worry not, *mon amie*,' Léon said, spreading his broad wings. 'The moon is not high yet and the Venteux Mountains are close. We will have our friends back with us soon and together, we will return to Noah's Ark in the hollow!'

Leaping from the tree branch, he burst into the night sky, closely followed by GI Joe. Henri cantered after the birds through the trees, with Pip tightly clutching the fur on the crown of his head.

It wasn't long before she felt the earth change beneath Henri's hooves and he slowed, climbing the steep verge of the Venteux Mountains with his breathing becoming heavier. As they made ground, the full moon climbed into a clear starry sky and Pip looked over to the rich valleys filled with trees below, and gazed at the towering peaks, grazing the clouds in the distant gloom.

A strange silence crept over the forest as the stag stopped wide-eyed, with his ears fixed ahead of him.

'What is it?' Pip said.

'Over there,' Henri whispered with a nervous shudder of his tail, 'Look.'

Ahead, the forest cleared into a huge, barren rectangle. At each corner, a tall, timber guard tower loomed over the camp, each with eight small windows staring into the darkness and searchlights poised upon their frames. They were linked by a tall fence woven with a web of jagged metal fangs, and inside the enclosure, seventeen black outbuildings stood in two lines. At the far end, a long, narrow chimney loomed above the biggest building in the camp.

'Stay here,' GI Joe cooed softly, perching for a moment on the stag as Léon hovered above. 'We'll survey the area.'

Climbing to the top of Henri's antlers, Pip watched the birds soar upwards and disappear through the shadowy treetops. Staring into the clearing, her eyes fell on a row of wheelbarrows standing in the middle of the camp and the fur on the back of her neck stood on end. She listened to the leaves whisper in the wind.

'Pssst,' GI Joe whispered, now swooping over their heads with Léon by his side. 'Regroup.'

Henri slowly stepped backwards into the cover of the forest, never taking his eyes off the strange place ahead. The birds landed silently on his antlers.

'Listen to me,' Léon whispered, his gold eyes flicking between them. He pointed his speckled wing to the rows of black outbuildings behind the barbed-wire fence. 'The human inmates of the camp are asleep in their barracks. When I was imprisoned here, they kept me in a dug-out hole in the ground under that one in the far corner, opposite the big chimney. The sharpest barbed wire, like the ones on top of the fence, are dragged over the hole, so no one can climb out and escape. Goliath Rats guard it too. I am sure Madame Fourcade, Hans and André will be there.'

'Goliath Rats,' Pip said. 'Like the ones Hans told us about?'

'They are savage, bloodthirsty devils,' Léon said, twitching his wings with unease. 'You must never let one come near you or it will be the last thing you do.'

'How did you escape from them?' Pip asked, fear drumming inside her chest as she spotted the shadow of an enormous rat creep beneath one of the outbuildings. It must have been twice the size of Hans and he was more than three times as big as she was.

'For interrogations, they take you out of the hole and inflict terrible suffering until you give them the information they want.' The eagle's feathers ruffled around his neck with anger. 'They tied me down and gnawed away at my legs, chewing them very slowly so I felt the worst pain possible. But I never surrendered and the moment they left me alone so they could decide the

237

rest of my torture, I pecked through the snare they had trapped me in.'

Pip's eyes fell on Leon's horribly crooked leg, deformed at the knee where his hooked beak had almost completely cut off his lower limb. Staring at the scars screaming across both his legs, she turned away in horror, seeing clearly where the Goliath Rats' teeth had slowly ground through his flesh to the bone.

'Don't worry liddle lady,' GI Joe cooed softly. 'You won't need to do anything like that. All you need to do is drag the barbed wire away from the hole. Then with some help, Madame Fourcade, Hans and André can climb out and escape.'

'OK,' Pip said, trying to stop her whiskers from trembling. 'Put me down, I'll run across the fence to the hole.'

'It's not that simple, *mon amie*,' Léon said. 'That fence around the camp is electrified. It will fry you alive if you touch it.'

'But I'm small. I can squeeze under it.'

'No, it's dug into the ground – we can't risk it. Even if you managed to pass through without touching the fence, Hans, Madame Fourcade and André are too big to do the same and you all need to slip through it as quickly as you can when you escape.'

'Then how do I switch it off? Tell me where it is and I'll do it now.'

'You need to go to the control room over there,' GI Joe cooed, pointing his wing at the building with the chimney at the far end of the camp. 'The switch pulses with electric current, so you will know which one to press. I will fly you to the roof, then all you need to do is climb inside and disable it. And you must be fast. If a human or anyone else sees you, they'll know the fence is not working and you won't have time to escape through it with the others.'

'Why can't you fly us out?'

'Because the guards will see you,' Henri said, pointing his head of antlers. 'Look at the towers at each corner of the camp.' Pip turned her gaze and shivered with fear. On top of each one, a huge bird was silhouetted in the moonlight, guarding the gloom like gargoyles snarling on a church roof. 'Those are the same sentry owls that captured Madame Fourcade, Hans and André. If they see you, they will capture you, if they don't kill you first.'

'Wait,' she said with a scowl. 'If they'll see me when I fly out, why won't they see me when I fly in?'

'Because I am going to distract them,' the eagle said,

his golden eyes glowing with determination. 'It should give you enough time to turn off the switch and run to the hole. Once you have released the others, you can escape together through the fence.'

'All right,' she said, staring at the control room and taking a deep, nervous breath. 'Let's do it.'

'Remember to keep your eyes wide open and on the ground,' GI Joe cooed. 'If the Goliath Rats see you, you will all be finished. Léon's diversion will buy you some time but we can't say how much.' He hopped from the stag's antlers to the base of his neck and, turning to Pip, a proud smile drew across his face. 'Are you ready, liddle lady?'

'I'm ready.' She nodded, but as she stepped towards him, she felt her limbs tremble with fear.

'I will meet you on the other side of the fence behind the chimney,' Henri said, turning to watch her climb up GI Joe's outstretched wing and clamber on to his back. 'It's as close to the hole as I can get so it won't be far for you to run. Then I will take us all home to the hollow.' His tail shuddered nervously. 'Good luck, young Pip.'

'Thank you, Henri,' she said with a lump in her throat. 'We'll see you soon.'

GI Joe leaped into the air from the stag's back.

Silently weaving in and out of the trees along the edge of the camp, they soon reached the branches behind the chimney. Swooping upwards, they waited there, watching with thumping hearts as Léon flew from the cover of the trees to the middle of the enclosure. Powerfully flapping his wings, the eagle landed on a wheelbarrow with a loud squawk, his golden eyes gleaming fiercely in the gloom.

CHAPTER TWENTY-FIVE

ESCAPE

The four eagle owls hooted in alarm and swivelled their heads with their ear tufts standing on end. Their orange eyes furiously narrowed as they spotted Léon obnoxiously shrieking on the wheelbarrow, pecking and clawing at its metal tray. Spreading their enormous wings, the owls leaped from their lookout posts one by one, gliding silently through the air with their cruel beaks and talons malevolently glinting in the moonlight. Gasping with horror, Pip held her breath as the first owl neared Léon's speckled head, gleefully hopping from wheelbarrow to wheelbarrow as if he did not know the danger he was in.

Screeching with murder, the owl opened its claws, eager to gore the eagle's flesh and taste his blood. But at the last moment, Léon leaped into the sky, leaving the owl's talons snapping on nothing but air. Screaming with rage, the four owls furiously gave chase, swiftly dodging and weaving through the sky. Léon was leading them to the far end of the camp, away from the chimney and into the forest beyond.

'It's working!' GI Joe whispered with triumph, watching the last flash of the owls' feathers disappear in the distance. 'Let's go.'

Jumping from the tree branch, they flew silently over the fence, which was humming with electricity. They glided past the tall chimney, silhouetted in the light of the full moon.

'Get ready to jump,' the pigeon whispered, now slowing above the control room, clearly lit with two gas lamps hanging on either side of the door. With every second, the roof loomed closer and Pip's chest thundered at the sight of a man moving in the approaching window. GI Joe glided downwards, grazing the top of the building. 'Three, two, one – GO!'

Pip leaped from his back. Hitting the roof with a rolling bump, she desperately grappled for a hold to stop her tumbling to the ground below. Latching her claws on to the edge of the roof and shivering with fright, she watched the last glimpse of the pigeon vanish into the nearby trees and drew a deep breath.

Below her, the muffled sound of men talking seeped from an open window. Carefully peering over the edge of the roof, she found the corner of the window frame jutting outwards. Wrapping her tail on the corner of a roof tile, she shuffled on her stomach and dangled over the open window before lowering herself to the upper edge of the frame. Craning her neck downwards to see into the room, she saw two men holding papers. One wore a long white coat and the other a sage-green uniform. Standing side by side, they organized newly arrived boxes of supplies from the train, stacked against the opposite wall.

'Gas?' one said.

'*Ja*,' the other said, making a tick mark on his paper.

'*Sehr gut. Munition?*'

'*Ja, Herr.*'

To their left, fixed beside the control room door, a circular red button gently pulsed with electricity, just as GI Joe had said. Pip looked around the room. The only way to get there was to cross the ground between the men's legs and climb up the power line. Feeling sick with fear, she carefully clambered across the wooden frame, using her claws to travel down its vertical edge to the window sill below. Keeping her eyes on the men, she lowered herself inside the room, climbing down the timber walls to the cold cement floor. Holding her breath, she crouched as motionless as the rows of umbrella handles she had once hidden behind inside the umbrella shop and, staring up at the men with her heart clamouring in her ears, she slowly edged towards their black leather boots.

'*Wo sind die Drogen?*' the man in the white coat asked, bristling with impatience.

Pip froze behind his foot as he looked from side to side.

'*Hier, Herr Doktor,*' the man in uniform said, turning away and stepping to the boxes in the corner.

As the other man followed, Pip scrambled to the power line on the opposite side of the room. After a careful glance at the men, she scaled the wire to the red circle buzzing with electrical power. Pressing it with all her strength, the button sank slowly into the wall. Hearing it click, she smiled, watching its glow instantly dim and disappear. With one last look at the men safely at the other end of the room, she hurried back down the wire to the floor. Racing to the control-room door as fast as she could, she squeezed through the gap under it and stepped into the night.

The full moon shone brightly above the camp, casting shadows across the ground. Keeping watch beside the neighbouring barracks stood a monstrous Goliath Rat with gleaming red eyes. Beyond it, Pip spied the tangled barbed wire glinting malevolently over the hole, exactly as Léon had said.

Looking desperately around the camp enclosure for cover, dread crept over Pip. To get to the hole, she must run from the control-room door to the barracks, completely exposed in the moonlight. Shivering from the tips of her whiskers to the end of her tail, she stepped forward. With one last scan of the sky to check for the owls, and a glance at the Goliath Rat, who had his back turned, she sprinted for the hole faster than she had ever run in her life.

But just as she reached the barracks' shadowy underbelly, the Goliath Rat's ears cocked. Pip darted behind the barbed wire, hardly daring to breathe. Seeing and hearing nothing but the nearby trees rustling in the breeze, the Goliath Rat scuttled away.

'Hans!' Pip whispered, staring through the metal thorns into the black hole, but there was no sign of life. Grabbing the barbed wire in her paws, she dragged it backwards in jangling tugs. 'Madame Fourcade!'

A gasp of fear was uttered below.

'They're back!' Terrified voices began muttering to each other.

'Be strong.' Pip's ears pricked up as she recognized Madame Fourcade's voice. 'Your spirit is your strongest weapon. Never let them take it away from you, no matter how badly they hurt you.'

Suddenly Pip could move no further. Gritting her teeth, she pulled the tangled mass of barbed wire with all her strength, but it was no use. The wire stubbornly remained unmoved, only revealing a narrow gap between its thorns and the hole below. Peering over the edge, three mice, two rabbits, a rat, three beavers and a hedgehog met her gaze.

'Pip!' Hans cried in a delighted whisper. 'What are you doing here?'

'I'm saving you!' She smiled. 'Hurry, climb out!'

'Quickly,' Madame Fourcade said, nudging the animals around her. 'Go! Go!'

A young, trembling rabbit was the first to clamber upwards, helped by the others lifting her from below. Pip grabbed her paw through the wire and pulled, trying to ignore the pain burning through her fur as the barbed wire ripped into her skin.

'Stop! Please stop!' the rabbit cried, wincing in agony and jerking her head away from the sharp gap in the barbed wire. Desperately shaking her head, a tear ran down her cheek and across the length of a whisker. 'I can't do it. The thorns are too sharp and thick.'

Feeling panic thunder inside her chest, Pip snatched the wire in her paws and frantically tugged once more, but again it would not move. The animals below looked at one another, muttering in dismay.

'Help me up,' Madame Fourcade said, and immediately the animals lifted her. Pip leaped for her paw and stared into the hedgehog's brown eyes, glistening with determination in the darkness. 'Pull, Pip! And don't let go!'

Madame Fourcade's prickles flattened all over her body. With the help of Pip from above and the animals from below, she slowly dragged herself upwards, quietly yelping in discomfort as she squeezed through the narrow gap in the tangled barbed wire. A long, painful minute brought her to Pip, breathlessly gulping the night air with relief.

'We must move this wire!' Madame Fourcade said, leaving no time to collect herself. Grabbing the wire in her paws, she heaved with all her strength, but it only jangled metallically. Letting it go, her tawny brow furrowed in despair. 'There must a way to move this thing!'

'Look!' Pip said, pointing to the ground where the thorns had latched into the earth. 'It's the teeth, they're stuck!'

They swiftly burrowed about the wire with their front claws.

'Well done, *chérie*!' the hedgehog cried as they triumphantly pulled it free from the hole. 'We've done it!'

'Hurry,' Pip whispered, lying on her stomach and reaching down for the animals' paws below. 'Climb up, we must get out of this place!'

One by one, the animals helped each other out into the night. Soon all ten prisoners cowered nervously alongside Pip under the barracks. She stared out into the camp with twitching whiskers, carefully keeping watch for Goliath Rats guarding the ground.

'What now, Pip?' Hans asked, stepping to her side. He had been the last animal to clamber out of the hole, having helped every creature out before him.

In the shadows, Pip's eyes fell on fresh scratches and bruises throbbing on his scarred face and neck. Madame Fourcade and the others had similar marks over their bodies.

'We run and escape through the fence over there,'

250

she whispered, pointing her paw to the trees behind the closest fence, where the stag had promised to meet her. All the animals turned to look at the fence standing a few metres away. 'Henri and GI Joe are waiting for us.'

'What about the owls?' Madame Fourcade said.

The other animals nodded nervously and craned their necks to get a view of the sky.

'Léon has tricked them into the forest, but we must hurry, they could be back at any minute.'

A sudden clatter of wings silenced them all. Exchanging a frightened glance with Hans and Madame Fourcade, Pip peered out into the camp. A white bird had landed on the ground next to a Goliath Rat prowling under the neighbouring barracks. Recognizing each other at once, they began speaking in a language Pip did not understand.

'It's Lucia!' she squeaked in surprise, seeing the pigeon's face in full view. 'What's she doing here?'

'She's talking to the guards in German.' Hans growled. 'She's telling them about Noah's Ark coming to save us.'

'A friend can be a traitor,' the hedgehog said, clenching her fists with fury.

'It was her, wasn't it?' Pip said after a pause, her mind

racing with memories of the bitter row in the hollow under the fallen tree. 'Lucia sabotaged Operation Popeye!'

As she spoke, the Goliath Rat's cruel, blazing red eyes fell on the animals cowering above the hole. Throwing its head back, it cried out its alarm in a snarling roar.

'Run!' Hans said, pushing Pip and the others out into the night. 'Go! Now! Run for your lives!'

CHAPTER TWENTY-SIX

THE FIGHT

Pip bounded into the cold, bright moonlight with Hans, Madame Fourcade and the other animals by her side. The jagged web of spikes inside the fence loomed over the ground ahead, casting long, sharp, shadows that reached out to snare everything that crossed its path. Daring to look behind her, Pip's heart hammered against her ribs as she saw the Goliath Rat spit with fury and sprint after them from the neighbouring barracks. Beyond it, many more Goliath Rats now hurried across the camp, growling murderously as they raced towards the fence with alarming speed.

'They're gaining on us!' Pip cried, and at once each animal running alongside her panted, trying to run faster across the ground.

'Don't look back!' Henri bellowed, leaping out from the cover of the trees behind the fence and anxiously stamping the ground with his hooves. 'Run! Run as quickly as you can!'

GI Joe burst out from the treetops. Charging over the fence and swiftly diving through the air, he swooped to Pip, Hans and Madame Fourcade leading the sprint on the ground.

'Quickly, grab hold of me!' he cried, flying alongside them.

Pip hurled herself to him, wrapping her arms about his neck, while Madame Fourcade and Hans each caught him by a leg. The pigeon beat his wings with all his strength and climbed slowly into the air above the beavers, mice and rabbits sprinting in terror for the fence.

'What happened?' GI Joe panted.

'Lucia's an Axis spy!' Pip cried. 'She's the one who sabotaged the plan to destroy the bridge! She's here! And she knows the Goliath Rats – she's just warned them we were coming to rescue Hans and Madame Fourcade!'

'What?' the pigeon said. 'But that's impossible. Luey is one of us.'

'We saw her with our own eyes, GI!'

'How can she even be here? We left her with Noah's Ark in the hollow.'

'It's her, GI,' Hans said, jumping with Madame Fourcade from the pigeon's legs to the Henri's back, who was now standing beneath them. 'I'm sorry, it's been her all along.'

'It can't be,' GI Joe cooed, landing beside them and shaking his head with disbelief as Pip clambered off his body. 'I know her. She wouldn't do this.'

'If you don't believe us,' Madame Fourcade growled, 'then look for yourself! Lucia is one of them!'

GI Joe turned and, seeing her white feathers flying swiftly across the camp in the bright moonlight, his beak fell open in shock. Sentry eagle owls flanked her on both sides while another two glided closer to the ground, soaring through the air together above the Goliath Rats chasing the terrified animals.

'Maybe she's their prisoner,' he cooed desperately, cocking his head with confusion and spreading his wings. 'Then she's in trouble – I gotta save her.'

The stag shook his antlers and angrily stamped the ground with his hooves.

'No, GI!' Madame Fourcade said, leaping on to his wing. 'You cannot go back in there to save Lucia. She is the enemy and they'll kill you. It's because of her that we are here. Don't you see? Her weapon was to make you care about her! She's a traitor! She fooled us all!'

'But Luey—'

'No, GI! If she's with them, she believes in their evil ways – in killing, in torturing and in having power at all costs.'

'I can't believe it, she's—'

'Listen, friend,' Hans said urgently, staring earnestly into the pigeon's amber eyes. 'Look at us!' He pointed his paws to the other injured prisoners, sprinting on the other side of the fence. 'See the scars on our bodies and the stumps where their tails once were. Think of Léon, think of me – think of all the suffering you have seen during this war! Lucia is not who you think she is!'

There was a pause as the pigeon stared back at his mate, pursuing the petrified beavers, mice and rabbits across the ground. Slowly his eyes narrowed with rage.

'Then she can't get away with this,' he said, his feathers furiously ruffling all over his body.

'We have to do something!' Pip said, watching the Goliath Rats and the owls snarling at the other animals' heels. 'Run!' she cried, cupping her paws around her mouth. 'Run as fast as you can!'

But it was hopeless. The owls were the biggest birds she had ever seen. Each beat of their enormous wings propelled them forwards more powerfully than any animal running across the ground.

Pip marched to the pigeon and grabbed his wing in her paws, ready to climb on to his back. 'We can't stay here and watch them die. We have to help them!'

'No, Pip!' Hans said, dragging her from the pigeon's wing, firmly handing her to Madame Fourcade and jumping on the pigeon's back himself. 'This is not your fight. *We* must put an end to this.'

'Shhh, Pip,' the hedgehog hushed, tightening her grip around the little mouse struggling to get out of her grasp. 'Let them go.'

'No!' Pip cried, feeling the sting of tears in her eyes. 'Please! I can help, I know I can!'

'You have already helped us so much,' Hans said. 'Let us do what we need to do.'

'Don't worry, liddle lady,' GI Joe cooed, spreading his wings and plumping his chest feathers. 'We're gonna make them pay!'

With that, they burst upwards from the stag's back and charged into the sky. Breathless, Pip watched them hurtle over their heads and soar into the fight, outnumbered by five birds to one.

Seeing an owl swoop perilously close to one of the escaped mice, GI Joe and Hans torpedoed downwards. As its monstrous talons opened like a gaping jaw around its prey, the mouse squealed, hearing the owl and the pigeon squawk and clash violently behind her.

'Yes!' Pip cried with Henri and Madame Fourcade, watching the owl tumble in a heap on the ground. 'Run!' she shouted to the terrified animals nearing the fence. 'Keep going! It's not far now!'

GI Joe and Hans soared over the camp. Seeing the attack on its mate, the neighbouring owl narrowed its orange eyes in fury. Swivelling its head away from the beavers, mice and rabbits sprinting for the fence, it suddenly changed direction and charged at GI Joe with a fierce burst of its wings. He swiftly beat his own and desperately weaved through the sky, struggling to outrun the talons snapping at his tail feathers.

'They've reached the fence!' Madame Fourcade gasped, clasping her paws together with joy. 'Look!'

'That's it!' Pip cried, jumping up and down on the stag's back with triumph, watching the animals slowly navigate the thick web of barbed wire.

'Come, friends!' Henri said, dipping his head to the

fence. The animals panted, travelling as swiftly as they could through the metal barbs. 'I will take you home!'

'Watch out!' the stag bellowed a moment later, stamping the ground in alarm as a clatter of wings sounded overhead.

Above them, Lucia and two eagle owls flexed their fearsome claws and plummeted through the air as Pip and Madame Fourcade ducked, cowering in small balls on Henri's back. Swooping back upwards with empty talons, Lucia and the owls arced through the sky. Screeching furiously, they torpedoed again, diving at the stag's eyes and nose with their beaks and claws. Swiping his antlers from side to side in pain, Henri suddenly reared upwards. As he thwarted their attack with his front hooves, Pip cried out with fright and stumbled, desperately grappling for something to hold.

'No!' Madame Fourcade yelled, scrambling for her, but it was too late. Grazing the hedgehog's fingers with her own, a terrible lurch snatched Pip's paws from under her. As she tumbled through the air, a cold, pink, waxy talon closed around her and lifted her into the sky.

'Let me go!' Pip cried, fiercely struggling inside the bird's claws. Looking up, Pip laid eyes on the white pigeon and gasped in horror. 'Lucia! How could you do this to us!'

'We are not so different, you and me,' the pigeon cooed calmly, speaking in her true German voice as she swiftly flew beside the sentry owls towards the smoking chimney. Appalled, Pip stared at her with fury racing over her fur, unable to believe she was the same pigeon she had met inside the hollow. 'I am an orphan like you, Pip. The Nazis saved me when I lost everything, just like they are going to save you.'

'We're nothing alike! I'd die before I'd join the Nazis! You're a liar and a traitor, Lucia! We will never forgive you for doing this to Noah's Ark.'

'What do you care, Pip?' she cooed, and her blue eyes bitterly narrowed. 'You and your umbrella are not real members of Noah's Ark.'

'I'm more of a member of Noah's Ark than you'll ever be!'

'A silly dream for a stupid little mouse kitten.'

'I'd rather fight and die with Noah's Ark than live in the nightmare of an Axis world!'

'Whatever you may think –' Lucia smirked – 'you'll thank me when you see what's going to happen next.'

Pip looked down into the camp below and blinked with confusion. The Goliath Rats and the sentry owls had stopped chasing the animals picking their way through the barbed-wire fence. Now they raced in the opposite direction, towards the control room.

'No!' Pip cried, thrashing inside the white pigeon's grasp. 'You can't turn the fence back on! They'll be fried alive!'

'The sooner you realize you cannot beat us,' Lucia snarled, crushing Pip inside her talons and smiling, hearing the little mouse choke in her claws, 'the sooner you'll tell us everything you know about Churchill's Secret Animal Army. Before long, you'll join us too. We'll be sisters once again, Pip, you'll see.'

Pip's mind raced, thinking of a way to escape. Gasping for air, blood ringing inside her ears, she lurched forwards, trying to sink her teeth into the pigeon's fist, but Lucia only squeezed her harder. Feeling her consciousness ebb away, Pip saw the faces of Mama and Papa in the umbrella shop and everyone she had met since the bomb blast in London: Dickin, Bernard Booth, Madame Fourcade, Hans, GI Joe, Henri, Léon and Noah's Ark, all fighting for freedom. No matter what the enemy did to her, she would sooner die than tell their secrets, and as the world turned black, Pip's last desperate thoughts were searching for a way to help the others.

'Leave her alone!' Léon squawked, diving headlong

into the pigeon
in an explosion
of white and
speckled
feathers.

Lucia
shrieked in
alarm, feeling
the eagle's powerful
golden claws snap around
her throat. Wide-eyed with panic, she frantically beat
her wings and opened her talons to slash at Léon's chest,
sending Pip plummeting through the sky.

'We gotcha, liddle lady!' GI Joe cried, swooping
under her.

'It's all right,' Hans said, catching her in mid-air and
dragging her up on to the pigeon's back. Pip's eyes
fluttered open. Throwing her paws round the rat's neck,
she hugged him as tightly as she could.

'Thank you,' she said, trembling in his arms.

'Dear, brave little Pip,' he said, drawing her close. 'I
won't let anything happen to you.'

Pip looked over his shoulder and her chest tightened
with fear, seeing Léon and Lucia somersault through

the sky, ripping one another's feathers with their bloody beaks and claws.

'Hurry,' Pip said, desperately pointing at the Goliath Rats nearing the control room. 'They're going to turn the fence back on. Everyone will die if we don't stop them now!' But GI Joe raced in the opposite direction. 'You're going the wrong way!' she cried, pointing to the control room. 'Stop! We need to go that way!'

Ignoring her, GI Joe burst forward over the fence. A few seconds brought him back to Madame Fourcade and the stag, encouraging the beavers, mice, rats and rabbits slowly picking their way through the barbed wire.

'This isn't a job for you,' Hans said, peeling Pip off the pigeon's back and placing her into the hedgehog's open arms. 'It's too dangerous, Pip. They'll stop at nothing to capture you and I'll never forgive myself if that happened. I want you to find your family and get the umbrella to Italy.'

'But you're coming with me. Then you're going back to Bavaria.'

'That's right,' Hans said as his brow furrowed. His handsome, scarred face softened and her heart swelled in her chest, seeing his eyes glisten in the moonlight. 'Help the others now,' he said, motioning to the animals clambering through the fence. 'We'll be back soon.'

'See you soon, liddle lady,' GI Joe said, giving her an affectionate wink. 'It's been a pleasure.'

Leaping from the stag's back, GI Joe and Hans stormed over the fence into the camp once more. Ahead of them, a sentry owl charged into Léon, still bitterly brawling with Lucia in the night sky. Tumbling in the air, the eagle immediately suffered another brutal blow from a second owl who had gleefully joined the fight. Helplessly watching Hans and GI Joe soar through the moonlight towards the fight, Pip's eyes filled with tears.

'Come on,' she said, firmly wiping a teardrop from her face as she watched the three mice clamber free of the barbed wire and race across the grass to the stag. 'Henri, we've got to help them up.'

The stag leaped to the fence and bowed his head to the earth. Hurrying down his neck to the ground and grabbing the trembling animals by the paws, Pip and Madame Fourcade pulled each one through the last tangles of the fence and guided them up the stag, now kneeling and resting his chin on the ground. The rabbits also raced up Henri's head and along his neck to his back, where they huddled together in terror, watching the battle in the camp intensify.

Behind the fence, GI Joe and Hans swooped above the Goliath Rats nearing the control room. Diving fearlessly through the sky with his teeth and claws bared, Hans landed on the back of the leading Goliath Rat. The other rats pounced on him and GI Joe soared upwards, targeting only Lucia. Rocketing into her with all the strength he possessed, he threw her from her savage perch on Léon, still struggling against her and four sentry owls. Lucia was knocked senseless by the blow. Tumbling through the sky in a vicious clatter of wings, the pigeons torpedoed into the two gas lamps hanging either side of the control-room door. The glass shattered on the timber wall in a grim burst of flame.

'GI!' Pip squeaked, desperately searching for him in the fire that was quickly spreading up the building beside Hans, still fiercely brawling with the Goliath Rats on his own.

'Pip!' Madame Fourcade cried firmly, pulling the last beaver free of the fence before clumsily clambering up Henri's muzzle with her short legs. She came to a standstill on top of his head and looked down at the umbrella mouse, still on the ground. 'Pip! Come on!'

But Pip didn't hear her as she watched a Goliath Rat

snarl and hurl Hans on to his back as two more sprang on him.

GI Joe suddenly burst into the fray from the flames. Beating his blackened wings with all his might, he charged into one Goliath Rat and a moment later it lay motionless on the ground.

'Pip!' Henri bellowed. 'Climb up now! We must take cover in the woods!'

Clambering up the fur of the stag's cheek, she joined the hedgehog perched between his ears. As he lurched forward and stood, Henri's head rose above the ground and Pip's mouth fell open as she gained a clearer view of the fight behind the fence.

The fire was now racing over the roof of the control room to the neighbouring barracks and clouded the moon with thick, black smoke. As the flames spread over the walls the barracks door's hinges buckled in the heat. It burst open and a bony man wearing baggy trousers with a matching striped shirt appeared in the broken doorway, kicking the smouldering timber away. Looking directly at the fence, he sprinted out of the building with a group of other men. As they ran, a voice shrieked with anger from a guard tower. Suddenly a large, bright shaft of light flashed into the gloom. A moment later, shots rang out into the night and two owls swooping to attack Léon were caught in the crossfire and jerked in the sky before dropping lifelessly to the ground.

'We need to get out of here,' the stag said, diving into the cover of the forest. 'Now!'

'But what about the others?' Pip said, looking back at Hans, GI Joe and Léon fighting the owls and the rats silhouetted against the fire, which was spreading wildly over the smoking chimney and surrounding buildings.

More men were spilling out of their barracks and racing through the beams of the searchlights across the camp. Behind them, guards hurried into the moonlight and lifted rifles to their shoulders. As a storm of gunfire thundered across the night, Pip and the other animals drew each other close, hearing bullets hiss into the trees about them. The escaped men were leaping through the barbed wire and scaling the fence even as the metal thorns clawed at their baggy clothes. Some were already vanishing into the forest.

'These poor men will be hunted, and we cannot risk the humans discovering us too,' Madame Fourcade said urgently.

'But we can't leave without them!' Pip sobbed.

267

'This is war, *ma petite chérie*. GI, Hans and Léon are soldiers fighting for our freedom and so are we. We must get everyone to safety so we can redouble our efforts and weaken the enemy. All of us dying here means fewer soldiers on the ground at a time when we need them the most. They know that better than anyone.'

Pip nodded reluctantly and a terrible knot of guilt formed in her chest, even as she accepted Madame Fourcade was right.

'Don't worry, *chérie*. Have faith. They will catch us up when they can.'

'Hold on, everyone!' Henri bellowed, swiftly turning around as all the animals on his back grabbed large tufts of his fur in their paws.

As the stag galloped forward, Pip looked over her shoulder at her friends battling with all their strength and courage. Feeling her heart splinter, she wept, unable to tear her eyes away from them. It was then that a huge explosion rocked the air around them. The control room disappeared in a thunderous white blast and lit up the surrounding forest in a fearful orange blaze.

CHAPTER TWENTY-SEVEN

THE CHOICE

On their return to the hollow under the fallen tree, Noah's Ark celebrated their friends' rescue, with Madame Fourcade and Henri recounting what had happened long into the night. Hailed as a hero, Pip's cheeks glowed scarlet and pink as the woodland creatures threw her into the air, and soon tales of the little umbrella mouse and the great escape spread far and wide, inspiring courage in all animals fighting for freedom from Hitler's snare.

Reunited with the umbrella, Pip felt a great cold struggle she had not experienced before. In the beginning, all that mattered was that she and the umbrella reached Gignese, just like Mama and Papa had wanted. But now it wasn't so simple. Not only had the war taken everything from her, it had changed everything she knew. It had shown her the kindness and the brutality of animals and human beings. She had seen cruelty and bravery, selfishness and self-sacrifice, and to live the same life inside the umbrella now made little sense to her. But she was an umbrella mouse. She also belonged in the Gignese museum with the only family she had left in the world.

As the days passed, Léon, GI Joe and Hans did not come home, and a silence fell on Noah's Ark. None felt the sorrow more than Pip, who had lost too much since the bomb had hit James Smith & Sons.

Without Hans, she had never felt more alone, and the journey to the umbrella museum seemed impossible. Her heart throbbed with guilt every time GI Joe and Léon entered her mind, wishing she could have done something to save them. To leave Noah's Ark and travel to Gignese now felt like a betrayal.

One breakfast a few days after their return, the bullfinch operating the crystal radio concealed in the leafy upper boughs of the hollow, looked up and ripped the headphones from his silky black and coral head.

'Madame Fourcade!' he cried, urgently fluttering to the ground and handing the hedgehog a scribbled note.

'I have an important message from Bernard Booth.'

'Let me see,' Madame Fourcade said, poring over the message with twinkling eyes. '*C'est sensationnel!*' She smiled broadly. 'Our umbrella mouse is being awarded the George Cross for acts of the most conspicuous courage in circumstances of extreme danger.'

A little cry of delight echoed from the woodland creatures and, clapping their feathers and paws together, they turned to the little mouse with pride glimmering across their faces. Warmth spread over Pip's fur as she looked at her new friends, recognizing the flame for freedom burning inside them and knowing only capture or death could tear them apart. She still couldn't believe Hans, Léon and GI Joe were really gone, and, gazing at the umbrella, she felt the right decision thump in her heart.

'Madame Fourcade,' Pip said, stepping away from the umbrella, 'I want to stay with Noah's Ark and fight with you until the end of the war.'

'But what about your umbrella, *ma petite chérie*?' Madame Fourcade said, blinking with surprise.

'I am the last surviving Hanway mouse of Bloomsbury Street and I must honour all the other Hanway mice before me and get my umbrella and myself to the museum in Italy where it belongs with my mother's family. But I owe it to all future umbrella mice to fight so that they can live in a free world and I can't leave you when I know I can help end the war that's taken Hans, Léon and GI Joe from us.'

'You are forgetting something, *chérie*,' Madame Fourcade said, wrapping her paw around Pip's shoulders and drawing her close. 'We are your family too. And we must not lose hope that our friends will find their way back. It was a terrible night we will never forget and you showed great courage. We'll need it more than ever if we're going to win this war. I know they were very proud of you – as are we.'

The woodland creatures nodded in agreement.

'Of course, after everything you have done for us,' the hedgehog continued, 'we will help you get to Italy whenever you wish. I promise we will never risk the umbrella's safety, and after we win the war, we will take you to Gignese with victory ringing in our ears! And the Allied armies are moving fast. We do not think it will be much longer before we battle for Paris and free her from the Axis snare. Then all roads lead straight to Berlin and Hitler will fall! Finally the war will be over and the world will be free. There are more adventures waiting for us, you'll see – and you'll love Paris, it's the most beautiful city in the world!'

'But we don't know who will win the war.'

'You must have faith that good will triumph, *ma petite chérie*. Otherwise, what are we fighting for?'

Pip looked into the faces of Noah's Ark and every creature smiled. What she was sure had been an ending had suddenly turned into a new beginning.

CHAPTER TWENTY-EIGHT

SURVIVOR

Deep in the wilds of the Venteux Mountains, bony men dismantled the remains of the southern border of the Nacht und Nebel camp, carting the ruins across the barbed-wire enclosure under the malevolent gaze of Nazi guards. Swept aside, the burned remains of rats and birds tumbled together past the tattered shoes shuffling along the ground and merged into a large pile of cinders and ash. Shovelled into a wheelbarrow, a small feathered body landed on the debris with a thump.

Its amber eyes snapped open and darted fearfully from left to right, its heart thundering beneath its ribs. Gasping for air, the bird mustered all the strength it possessed and, stretching its blistered wings, leaped unsteadily into the air, leaving a trail of soot lingering on the breeze as it turned for home.

AUTHOR'S NOTE

The Umbrella Mouse began around my twelfth birthday. My mother was in hospital and I was having trouble concentrating on a school project, writing a fictional interview with an inspirational person. Seeing me struggle, my father told me a story about my grandfather, a courageous RAF pilot who had been shot down over France in WWII and was rescued by villagers fighting with the French Resistance. During his escape, a teenage girl led him across a minefield in the dead of night, placing white handkerchiefs on the ground so he could navigate his way safely through the gloom. A number of those that helped him were killed by the military police shortly afterwards.

I can't remember what mark I got in that school project, but what I took from it was a strong interest in WWII, and the knowledge that stories could give me comfort and escape.

Fifteen years later, I was living in London with an English Literature degree and an ambition to become a children's author. One morning on my commute to work, I read some statistics revealing how little young people knew about the two world wars.

Remembering my grandfather, I began to research the French Resistance and as I read accounts of spies using secret messages, gadgets and invisible ink, I found betrayal, daring escapes and heroic sacrifice on almost every page. I was gripped by The Imperial War Museum's *British Spy Manual* and Marie-Madeleine Fourcade's memoir, *Noah's Ark*. She was about my age when she became the leader of 'The Alliance' – a vast intelligence network of 3,000 men and women fighting the German occupation of France. Not only was she a woman of authority living in a man's world, she was also the mother of two young children that she put into hiding, so she could risk her life to help the cause. She assigned her members animal codenames, earning them the title 'Noah's Ark', and she escaped capture twice – once by squeezing through the bars of her cell. *She* was my eureka moment and I chose two key members of Noah's Ark who had moved me the most to write about: Madame Fourcade as 'Hedgehog' and her close ally 'Eagle', the group's tragic hero, Commandant Léon Faye.

With anthropomorphism decided, more research led me to the extraordinarily resilient pigeons awarded the Dickin Medal that honours gallant animals fighting alongside humans in war. On reading Peter Hawthorne's

The Animal Victoria Cross and Evelyn Le Chene's *Silent Heroes*, a wealth of real-life animal heroes suddenly emerged, and as well as GI Joe and Bernard Booth's army of pigeons in London, Dickin also belongs to this group. Named after the medal, he resembles Rip, London's first search and rescue dog, and his handler Mr King appears with him. Maureen Waller's *A Family in Wartime* was a valuable resource when writing their scenes.

Lucia is based on the WWII pigeon POW, Lucia di Lammermoor, but I must add that there is no evidence to suggest she was *anything* other than heroic. Hans is inspired by Hans Scholl, a founding member of the German resistance group, 'The White Rose', who was executed in 1943 with his sister Sophie for their opposition to the Nazi regime. Lastly, the young shop customer in Chapter One is influenced by one of my favourite authors, Judith Kerr, as a tribute to her life and work.

A number of locations have been fictionalized for geographic and timeline purposes. The Nacht und Nebel camp is based on France's only concentration camp, Natzweiler-Struthof in the Vosges Mountains, and refers to the codename for Hitler's secret 'Night and Fog' order that was issued in response to the increased activity of resistance networks. Those arrested were either shot or taken to concentration camps. Their doom was deliberately clouded in mystery and a number of Noah's Ark members, including Léon Faye, suffered this fate.

The fire at the end of the book never occurred at Natzweiler-Struthof and is influenced by the Treblinka concentration camp in Poland where 200 prisoners revolted and escaped during a fire on 2nd August, 1943.

Finally, my heroine, Pip, came to me on a train during a wet and windy morning in December. As I cursed myself for forgetting my umbrella, I stared out of the window and watched the raindrops race across the glass. They somehow reminded me of mice darting across the floor (something I knew well from my student days in London) and I wondered what it would be like, to live inside an umbrella. With the chug of the train, my thoughts drifted to James Smith & Sons Umbrellas, a shop that I often walked past, and a quick search led me to the only umbrella museum in the world, in Gignese, Italy.

And so began my belief in intrepid umbrella mice that have made my dreams come true. Like them, I never knew what I was capable of until I tried.

ACKNOWLEDGMENTS

Every day, I pinch myself that this book has happened. When I started writing it on my phone during my daily commute on the London Underground, I loved it so much that I would often miss my stop. It was my first attempt at a novel and I never thought it would come this far. And it wouldn't have if it weren't for some brilliant people I have come to know. Please bear with my gushing.

Thank you to my super agent Chloe Seager at Northbank Talent Agency for believing in me. Not a day goes by that I don't feel grateful for your support, dedication and unparalleled sense of humour. My sincere thanks also go to the rest of the Northbank team and especially its founder, Diane Banks, for having faith in me and introducing me to the publishing world.

To my enormously talented editor, Lucy Pearse at Macmillan Children's Books, whose intelligence and imagination impressed me from the moment we met. I am eternally indebted to you for seeing something in *The Umbrella Mouse*. You've weaved editorial magic into its pages and I cannot thank you enough for making it the book that it is today. I've loved every minute.

To the superlative team at Macmillan Children's Books: Venetia Gosling for taking me on; PR wizards Jo Hardacre, Alyx Price and marketing ace Kat McKenna for getting the word out; to Tracey Ridgewell for designing a beautiful front cover and the insides. It's an honour to work with you all.

To the incredible illustrator, Sam Usher: you have brought my words to life in the most evocative way and the book would not be the same without you. Each image is a joy to behold and it's a privilege to share a page with you.

To Fraser Crichton for copy-editing and to Nick de Somogyi for proofreading, I really appreciate all the time you spent on my MS.

To Marie-Madeleine Fourcade and Léon Faye. I hope I have done your extraordinary stories justice. They deserve to be known everywhere.

To Clare Povey and James Rennoldson at Writers & Artists for their ongoing support and for introducing me to Cressida Downing, who taught me everything about the submission process. She was the first person to read my manuscript and believe in my mad idea about a mouse living inside an umbrella joining the French Resistance. Without her encouragement and editorial advice, I may have never quietened my crippling self-doubt and shown it to anyone, let alone a literary agent. So huge thanks to you, Cressi. We'll soon celebrate the book's publication over cocktails (as promised!)

To the authors, editors, booksellers and book bloggers who have already been so kind: to Michael Morpurgo, as one of your many mega-fans, I had an out-of-body experience when I read your quote for the book; to Gill Lewis, yours made my heart sing; to Fiona Noble for including me in your previews – I still feel light on my feet; to Mel Taylor-Bessent for inviting me to Authorfy – I have so many excited butterflies.

To the Imperial War Museum, I could not have written this book without your incomparable exhibitions and resources.

To James Smith & Sons Umbrellas in London, thank you for maintaining the original features inside your shop and supporting *The Umbrella Mouse*. I hope you keep your eyes peeled for intrepid mice!

To my husband, James, my best friend, my writing companion, my heart. Words cannot express how much you mean to me. I cherish every moment with you.

To my friends and family: thank you for your enduring support, kind ears and honest guidance.

To my parents, Tim and Lizzie, for always encouraging my siblings and I to be creative and for taking us on long family holidays exploring Scotland, Italy and Portugal, where we did very little but read books all day in the sun.

To Zoë, Matthew and Ed for *always* being there (and for suggesting the strapline, Zo) and to Auntie Banana: thank you for your excellent advice.

I must also apologize to my friends and family for the times I had to be absent from weddings, birthdays and gatherings because I was juggling jobs and novel-writing. I've learnt some lessons and I hope I won't have to do it again.

And to you, dear reader. I give you my deepest thanks for coming on Pip's adventures with me. I hope you'll join me for the next one.

ABOUT THE AUTHOR

Anna Fargher was raised in a creative hub on the Suffolk coast by an artist and a ballet teacher. She read English Literature at Goldsmiths before working in the British art world and opening her own gallery. *The Umbrella Mouse* is her first book, which she wrote on her phone's notepad during her daily commute on the London Underground. She splits her time between London and Suffolk, where she is often found exploring the coastline and marshlands under the huge East Anglian skies.

ABOUT THE ILLUSTRATOR

Sam Usher graduated from the University of West England and his debut picture book *Can You See Sassoon?* was shortlisted for the Waterstones Prize and the Red House Children's Book Award. He is particularly admired for his technical drawing skill and prowess with watercolour. Also a talented pianist, when he's not holding a pen and wobbling it at paper, you'll find him perfecting a fiendishly difficult piece of Chopin.